MILE HIGH
Book One of the
Men in Motion Series
G.A. HAUSER

MILE HIGH
Book One of the Men in Motion Series
Copyright © G.A. HAUSER, 2010
Cover art by Stephanie Vaughan
ISBN Trade paperback: 978-1449-5925-3-0

Second publication The GA Hauser Collection: February 2010

Chapter One

"Okay…let me go. I'll never catch my plane if you don't stop talking." Owen Braydon rubbed his face tiredly, looking down at his leather suitcase that sat by the front door. "Jenna, I have to go! Goodbye." Hanging up the phone, Owen made sure he had his keys and his plane tickets, then grabbed his bag and jogged out to his car. Checking the time on his watch, he cursed his ex-wife and her constant nagging even though they had been divorced for a year. If it wasn't for his daughter, Leah, he wouldn't be making the trip.

Trying not to be distracted by his frustration and anger, Owen drove to LAX in the traffic, mumbling profanity under his breath at his slow progress. Finally parked in the long-stay lot, he jogged to the check-in desk after locating his flight on the monitor. Handing the heavily made-up female clerk his ticket and checking his bag, at last he felt unencumbered, as if he could finally relax, and walked calmly through the security check-point.

Once he was on the other side of the metal detectors, seeing he did actually end up with a spare minute or two after all the rushing, he made for a lounge and sat at the bar.

"Can I have a glass of white wine, please?" He took a few dollars out of his wallet.

He sipped the crisp chardonnay, feeling some of the tension leave his body. Owen looked at his reflection in a mirror behind a wall of bottles of alcohol. Taming his hair and fixing his shirt collar, he straightened his back to improve his sagging posture and tried not to think about everything he had on his mind.

"Yes, I'd like a glass of that lager. The one on tap."

Owen turned his head to see a man ordering a beer beside him. Doing a quick appraisal, Owen estimated him to be in his mid-thirties, six-foot tall, and possibly nearing two hundred pounds of solid muscle. Looking away as the attractive man caught him staring, Owen returned his attention to his drink and checked on the time once more.

Sucking the rest of the wine down, he set a tip on the counter, then stood, intending on waiting at the gate until boarding. As he was about to leave, the handsome man, now seated at a small table with three high bar stools surrounding it, met his eyes. They smiled politely at each other. Owen wondered what his life story was. He often did that.

As people came and went around him, Owen invented their intimate details in his head. For example, the woman behind the desk at the check-in with her heavy make-up and long, painted nails. Well, she was simple to assess. At the clubs every night, getting tipsy, dancing wildly, her lipstick smeared on her face, until some poor fellow took pity on her and brought her home either to sleep or to screw.

The vignettes amused him. He didn't have what anyone would call an exciting life as an accountant, so why not live his fantasies and tell tales in his head to keep life that much more interesting?

As he walked down the crowded concourse to his gate, Owen tried to imagine the handsome man's story. *Well, he's so damn good looking he's either an actor or a model, has a gorgeous wife and a couple of kids, lives in a house in Beverly Hills. Or he's gay and has an Adonis named Sven, waiting for him naked in their private spa.*

Chuckling to himself, Owen hoped that the latter was the case. It made that handsome fellow more wicked and taboo, more interesting. And the thought of some ordinary man on the street being completely and utterly gay, always got a rise out of him. Though he'd never had a gay experience, he had always been curious what it would be like to dabble in the "dark side". Even while he was married, he had secretly admired the men on the television screen, allowed Jenna to watch shows that might have been threatening to the average husband, like romantic comedies or movies where her heartthrobs had nude scenes. In his head he'd say, "Oh yes", or "Yum!" at their naked torsos and bottoms, but kept his face straight for her and the public. He was a "happily married man" after all. *Tsch, tsch! Don't get caught drooling over naked men!* He smiled. "Well, you're not married any longer. Bring it on!" he joked with himself as if suddenly a hoard of attractive guys would come out of the woodwork and seduce him. He shook his head at the irony because he felt very ordinary, had a boring job, and was sadly approaching his late thirties. What could possibly happen this late in his life to make it exciting and fun? Nothing.

Seeing he still had a few minutes before the plane began boarding, Owen sat down with the crowd of exhausted patrons to linger until his assigned row was called.

That man from the bar approached their waiting area. Owen stared at the way he walked. Confident, masculine, solid, and very sure of himself. *Wow.* Owen felt his skin prickle. Whoever owned him must enjoy him. *What a fucking bod!*

When their eyes met again, Owen felt his face flush at that warm smile. It was as if drinking in the same lounge gave them something in common. Owen returned that amiable expression with more enthusiasm than earlier. He even nodded his head to give his greeting more authenticity. Again his internal dialogue took wing. *Where are you sitting, my handsome friend? In first class? Coach with the rest of us peasants? My row?*

It was good fun. Owen was relieved someone was there to pique his interest for the arduous two and a half hour flight.

As he gazed around the waiting area, he found nothing else of note. A very average looking bunch of human beings surrounded him; the usual assortment of crumpled businessmen, worn-out women with screaming, bratty children, and overweight tourists in gaudy prints who talked too much.

The boarding process finally began. Owen stood up with his pass in his hand, joining the droll line as the woman in a dark uniform checked their information before letting them through. Twisting around to see where his male friend was, he was happily surprised to see him standing in the same queue. *Well, at least you're close by.*

Moving down the narrow gangway to the opening of the airplane, Owen showed a flight attendant his ticket stub and was directed to his seat.

Finding it next to the window on the left side of the plane, Owen sat down and made himself comfortable, staring out at the runway and the action of loading luggage and departing flights.

After a few moments, he was about to pull a magazine out of the seat pocket in front of him when he noticed that handsome man sitting on an aisle seat one row up and diagonally from him. Again they caught eyes and smiled.

Hello! Oh, this just keeps getting better and better.

That gaze lingered; Owen was able to see those light eyes were blue. The man turned back around in his seat and took out a magazine to browse through.

Owen had to calm himself down. The tingles passing over his body amazed him. Stretching out his legs in the tight confines of the seat, Owen looked out at the tarmac again in order to gain some control. *Gay, gay...oh, yes, gay. You don't look at another man like that for no reason. Or...perhaps he just thought I looked familiar. Was that it? Did he think he knew me?*

Owen's spirit slightly deflated. Maybe the man just thought he looked like someone he knew. Maybe that was all it was.

The head flight attendant got on the intercom and began the monotone announcement of their destination, blah, blah, blah. Owen noticed them closing the cabin doors and was relieved he had a vacant seat next to him. Fastening his seatbelt, he flipped through a SkyMall magazine with little interest, thinking some of the contraptions were absurd. Two hundred dollars for ear-hair clippers and toe-jam cleaners!

The plane jolted slightly as it backed up. Owen stuffed the magazine into the pouch and made sure his mobile phone was off for the flight. Yearning to lie down and sleep, he looked down at his lap, his sky-blue faded jeans and his sensible leather shoes, wishing he could push the seat in front of him forward and move it ten inches away from his poor, aching knees.

They were next in line for take-off. The always-confident voice of the captain came over the PA and calmly told the staff to take their seats. From where he was sitting, Owen could see only part of the handsome man's left leg and left arm as it rested on his armrest. No wedding ring, but he did have a gold ring on his pinky finger. Was that another gay sign?

Owen felt the G-force from lift-off and waited for the plane to level out and the seatbelt sign to click off so he could get a cocktail.

The ding-ding of the signal finally sounded and Owen could see some movement in the front of the plane as the attendants got their cart loaded. Taking a five out of his wallet, Owen blinked in shock as the man he'd been eyeing moved out of his seat and sat right next to him in the vacant one.

"Hey," he whispered in a deep voice.

Owen was so shocked, he almost didn't answer. Completely agog at the boldness, he cleared his throat and croaked, "Hi."

"You mind if I sit here?"

"No! No. It'll be nice to have the company." Owen felt his skin cover with chills and his cock go rock hard at the overt act. *Wow!* Could his life finally be getting some excitement? Or was the accountant destined for boredom eternally?

Getting a closer look at this amazing man's face, Owen admired his square jaw, dark shaven stubble, incredibly blue eyes, and thick chocolate-colored hair that was long enough to cover his ears and brush his denim shirt collar. Owen lost himself on his sideburn, which was cropped short, halfway down his ear. Perfect. Absolutely perfectly groomed and smelling divine.

"I'm Taylor. Taylor Madison," the man said as he extended his right hand.

"Owen Braydon," Owen replied, taking that warm hand and squeezing it. The grip was electric and communicated something sexual as if they were screaming at each other their attraction.

"Business trip?" Taylor took back his hand slowly.

"No. Uh, I have a young daughter in the Denver area. I visit every weekend."

Nodding, Taylor looked down at Owen's lap. Owen wondered if he was checking his hand for a wedding ring, or maybe his crotch for a hard-on. He didn't know which but hoped Taylor liked what he found.

The attendants finally made it to their row with the cumbersome cart. "Would you like a drink?"

Owen nodded. "White wine, please."

"I'll take a beer, thanks." Taylor handed her a ten-dollar-bill and pushed Owen's hand away when he offered money.

As she set a small bottle of wine on Owen's tray table, he wondered if she realized there had been an empty seat next to him and now it was occupied. She didn't seem to care.

When she left, Taylor poured his beer into the provided glass.

Owen said, "Thanks, I'll get the next round."

Laughing softly, Taylor replied, "All right."

"So," Owen cleared his throat, trying not to sound nervous, "what's the reason for your flight?"

"I'm a project manager on a construction site." Taylor sipped his beer and licked his lip after.

Detecting a slight accent, Owen nodded, gazing at Taylor's mouth, trying to decipher where he was from. "You...you travel often?"

"I will be. The closer it gets to completion, the longer I have to stay." Taylor set the glass on the tray in front of him and boldly placed his hand on Owen's thigh.

Owen thought he would combust. It was so outrageous, so daring, so unbelievable, he froze under its heat. In his ear came a breathy whisper, "You're fantastic looking, you know that?"

Swallowing his anxiety, Owen knew he wasn't ugly, but *fantastic*? That was quite a compliment coming from a man who was Owen's ideal description of a male model. As the vision flashed through his mind of Taylor posing for designer briefs in front of a fashion photographer, under the concealment of the tray Taylor's hand caressed Owen's thigh muscle over his snug-fitting, faded blue denims.

"Shit. Can we get thrown off the plane for this?" Owen craned his neck up to see where the drink trolley had gone.

All Taylor did was chuckle softly.

Sucking the wine down so quickly it went to his head, Owen set the glass next to the empty bottle and snuck his hand on top of the one on his thigh, holding it tightly. Once Taylor had finished his beer, he placed Owen's empties on his own tray, folded Owen's tray up, and shook out a dark blue flannel blanket after taking it out of its flimsy plastic bag.

As Owen looked on in complete awe, Taylor pushed the arm up that was separating them, yanked the screen down over the window to provide some darkness, and spread the blanket over both of their laps. "Christ," Owen breathed, "you've obviously done this before."

Under his breath, Taylor replied, "Uh, no. I never have. I just figured it'd be best to be discreet."

"No shit!" Owen looked around but none of the other passengers appeared interested, too busy drinking their drinks and nibbling peanuts.

"Oh. Sorry. Was I getting the wrong vibe from you?" Taylor sat back from him.

"No!" Owen answered, then lowered his voice. "No. Right vibe, just a little nervous."

"Are you gay?"

"Uh…" Owen didn't know how to answer that question in order not to turn Taylor off. "How about bi-curious?"

A big grin appeared on Taylor's lips. "That'll work."

The stewardess appeared next to their row to clear the empty bottles. Owen was going to order them another round, but when Taylor clipped his tray back up behind the seat, Owen decided perhaps he had something else in mind. Something more enjoyable than booze.

The blanket was spread out neatly to cover both their laps.

Owen tensed when Taylor's left hand moved towards his crotch area. Frozen, not knowing how to react, Owen waited hoping no one was aware of what they were doing. Taylor caressed Owen's cock, his hot palm cupping it gently. Stifling a groan, Owen spread his legs wider in the tight space, truly astounded at what was going on under the blanket.

It was forward, wild, and had to be quick. They only had two and a half hours in the air. It wasn't as if they could have some long wooing courtship and relationship. This was a one-time act of groping that he was sure would be a fond memory once they had landed.

That hand managed to get his fly undone. The moment Taylor's fingertips hit the skin of Owen's pelvis, Owen closed his eyes in reflex and couldn't believe the sensation of thrills and chills coursing down his back and neck at this daring deed.

~

The minute Taylor felt how hard Owen was, he lit on fire. Taylor had spotted him at the check-in area in the terminal and had hoped Owen was going his way. When Taylor found him in the same waiting lounge, he couldn't believe his luck. The smiles, the lack of a wedding ring, it was too good to be true. The attraction he felt was immediate. Taylor considered himself picky when it came to men. He was sick of the cocky, self-absorbed types that only wanted what they could get and gave nothing. Owen seemed sweet and kind. His shyness was refreshing to Taylor. Shy, modest, and good looking? A rare combination indeed. Usually, the handsome ones were arrogant. Not this one. This man was gentle, almost bashful.

"Christ, you are amazing," Taylor hissed behind a clenched jaw. "I'll meet you in the bathroom."

"What?" Owen opened his eyes with a blink. "Bathroom?"

"Yeah. Wait a couple of minutes, then come back. Knock if they're both occupied to see which one I'm in."

~

As Taylor removed the blanket from his lap and unbuckled his belt, Owen quickly zipped up his fly. Panting in anxiety, he watched Taylor's tight ass as he climbed out of the confining seat and walked to the back of the plane. Owen couldn't catch his breath. What on earth was he doing? Was he totally insane? Nothing like this ever happened to him. He was the boring, down to earth type with no sense of adventure and too much anxiety to enjoy a wild fling. Or was he?

Waiting, checking his watch, Owen rubbed his face and kept asking himself what he was doing. "Oh, what the fuck. Life's too short." He tried to recall his last meaningless sexual encounter. Sadly, it was with his ex-wife and too long ago to remember. He didn't date. He had no time to date. Between work and his trips to Denver, when did he have time? Besides, who'd want to date a man with all his baggage—an ex-wife and a small daughter in another state? It was too much to ask of anyone.

Counting down in his head like a child about to play hide-and-seek, Owen felt he needed to give the correct amount of time between he and Taylor standing up. He unbuckled his seatbelt and boldly made his move to the rear of the plane. Peering at the faces who spied him as he went Owen wondered if anyone knew what the hell he was about to do. Did he?

Seeing the weary attendants busy in the galley behind the bathrooms, Owen almost chickened out. Both toilets were occupied. Swallowing for courage, he picked one out of the two and rapped on it. The door immediately opened, and he sighed with relief at getting the right one.

Instantly, Taylor dragged him into the miniature compartment and bolted the door. It was so tight they were standing an inch apart with Taylor's calves nudged against the commode behind him.

When Taylor's hands cupped Owen's face, Owen felt his skin burst into chills. Those lips were approaching. *I'm going to kiss a man! I'm about to kiss a man!* "Holy crap!" he said out loud before he realized it.

Taylor stopped right before their mouths connected and met Owen's eyes. "You don't want to do this, do you?"

Did he? Owen's heart was pounding like he'd just run a marathon, his skin was covered in goose pimples, and most importantly, his cock was throbbing so much it was painful. "I must want to because I'm so hard I could spurt."

Taylor's eyes lit up, and he broke up with laughter. Owen laughed with him at the same time as he was trying to shush him. It took a moment for them to calm down. "Oh, forget it. You only live once. Get over here."

"Over where? I haven't gone anywhere." Taylor kept laughing, pointing to the cramped space.

"I mean go ahead and kiss me." Owen stood nose to nose with Taylor, daring him.

Once again, Taylor cupped Owen's jaw gently, drawing Owen to his mouth.

The thoughts that passed through Owen's head were so numerous it made him dizzy. From the idea that no one in the world would believe he had done this, to the amount he was turned on, to the impulse of telling someone, or never telling someone, and reliving it when he was lying in his bed alone at night.

Clicking back to the present, absorbing the fact that a man, *yes, a man*, was kissing him, his tongue entering his mouth, Owen was so excited he wondered why he didn't act on that bi-curiosity previously. Of course, he had been married and wasn't the type to stray. So that answered that question.

Owen returned the favor by moving his tongue into Taylor's mouth. Shaking himself out of his stupid thoughts to actually enjoy the kissing, Owen boldly reached into Taylor's thick dark hair and drew him even closer, letting him know he was doing okay and all systems were go.

The plane's soft listing had them rocking side to side to keep their balance.

When Owen felt Taylor's hands go for the front of his jeans again, he parted from the kiss and looked down to watch.

"Okay?" Taylor asked.

"Okay... Ah, what are you going to do?"

"What do you want me to do?"

Owen looked back at the closed door. "How long you think they'll go before knocking and making sure nothing's going on?"

"Don't worry. They won't do anything until we get closer to Denver and have to return to our seats."

"You sure?" Owen had no idea why Taylor was so confident if he hadn't done this before.

Taylor stopped opening Owen's zipper. "You're too nervous. It's okay. I understand."

11

In the tight space the plane shifted again and Owen fell against Taylor's chest. Taylor set him upright.

"What were you going to do, you know, if I hadn't stopped you?" Owen didn't refasten his jeans, dying to know what was on offer.

"Suck it."

"Yeah?" Owen's heart skipped a beat. Jenna never did it. *The prude.* He'd heard every excuse in the book. "I don't want to, do I have to? You're so demanding! Can't we just do it nice?...waa waa..."

Owen wasn't going to miss an opportunity like this. *Get my dick sucked? Are you kidding me?* He'd have to pay a hooker hundreds of dollars for that, or worse, go to a bar and take home some drunken harlot. Oh, no. He much preferred this Hollywood model to do it for free. He opened his zipper, bracing himself on the close walls.

A wry smile found Taylor's face again. Sitting down on the closed commode, which was making some horrifying sucking sound on a constant basis that could bring a person to panic attacks, Taylor reached into Owen's briefs and exposed him. As if taking a moment to admire him, Taylor then opened his mouth.

Owen choked in astonishment. It was a dare! He didn't think Taylor would really do it! "Oh, holy shit...that feels so fucking good!" He heard a stifled chuckle. Looking down at Taylor, Owen couldn't quite believe what he was seeing, doing, or feeling. His brain went into overdrive. Not only was this his first blowjob in over a decade, it was from a man! *A man!*

"Uh, Taylor, you may want to back off, I'm getting close." Waiting, holding back for the poor guy, Owen was surprised when it seemed to excite Taylor even more. The pace quickened, the sucking grew stronger. Under his breath Owen warned, "I'm coming, I'm coming..." Then, knowing there was no turning back, Owen climaxed, pushing against the thin walls of the toilet, closing his eyes in a swoon. After a moment Owen opened them again, looking down at Taylor's bright, sparkling gaze. "Holy shit...that was unbelievable. I can't remember the last time someone did that to me."

"You're kidding? Oh, come on. You don't get your cocked sucked? Why the hell not? You're so fucking good looking."

Owen stared at Taylor while he stood back up, wiping his mouth with the back of his hand casually. Suddenly, Owen felt a strong attraction for Taylor that dug under the superficial layer of stranger sex. There was a warmth to him he was beginning to admire. His words were sincere and good-hearted. And even though he was amazing, Taylor didn't seem to own the conceit that men who looked like him usually did. "Your turn?" Owen asked bravely.

Smiling knowingly, Taylor replied, "I don't know if you're up for it. I've been with guys. I'm not a newbie."

"Look, I want to return the favor. I'm a fair-dealer, Taylor."

"It's okay."

"No. It isn't." Owen went for Taylor's tight jeans, pulling open the button and zipper.

Taylor looked down at Owen's hands pensively. "You...you want to just jerk me off?"

Owen stared at Taylor's face, then his body. *No, that's not a fair deal. I can do this. I will do this.* "I'll suck you."

"You sure? You don't have to just because—"

In the cramped space, Owen held onto Taylor's hips, and inch-by-inch, they traded places. Owen sat down on the closed seat, which was still gurgling and hissing loudly, and exposed Taylor's cock. It was huge. "Wow. I'm jealous."

"You have nothing to be jealous of. You have a fantastic body."

"Not like this. Man...you must be very proud of it."

"Change your mind?"

"Nope. I'm going for it. Wish me luck."

Taylor cracked up with laughter. "Good luck."

Licking his lips, staring at the engorged head of Taylor's penis, Owen knew it was a once in a lifetime chance, and he'd already decided on the *you only live once* principle. Besides, he'd gone this far already. Why turn back now? He opened his mouth and touched Taylor's cock to his lips. It was soft and spongy. A small sound of encouragement came from Taylor. Owen looked up at him for reassurance, then he shoved Taylor's cock passed his lips. As the size of it filled his mouth, Owen closed his eyes and held it tightly with his lips covering his teeth, trying not to scratch him. The plane listed and forced him to move forward, making the cock go deeper into his mouth. Once he found his balance again, Owen moved up and down its length, trying to decide if it was horrible or wonderful or someplace between the two.

~

Taylor was amazed at how bold Owen was, knowing damn well this was his first gay experience. Owen took Taylor's entire cock into his mouth, experimenting with his tongue. Taylor was impressed at the effort and soon forgot it was Owen's maiden foray into man on man loving and felt himself rising. "I'm getting close." Waiting for Owen to back off and finish the rest of the job with his hand, Taylor held back. But no move was made to disconnect. Shrugging, knowing he'd given fair warning, Taylor came, shivering down to his boots and closing his eyes. When he opened them and looked down, Owen was smiling at him proudly. "I did it. Ha!"

"Nice job!" Taylor fastened his jeans.

"I did it! I even swallowed. How cool is that?"

"Did you enjoy it?"

After a pause, Owen nodded. "Yes. I did."

"Good." Taylor checked himself out in the mirror, then asked, "You ready?" Owen nodded. "You go first. I'll be right there."

Nodding again, Owen opened the door, peeked out, and

14

left.

Taylor stared at his reflection in the mirror and whispered to it, "Oh, Owen, I know this is a one-time deal, but it sure would be cool to get to know you better."

~

Trying not to catch anyone's eye, Owen returned to his seat. The minute he was buckled in, the air-hostess leaned over to whisper something to him. About to hold up his hands and deny any claim that he was a pervert and should be thrown in jail, she asked, "Would you like your meal served now?"

"Oh." Seeing everyone else had their food and was digging in hungrily into the foil-covered trays, Owen, stuttered for a moment for an answer, when big beautiful Taylor appeared. The hostess moved aside, allowing Taylor back into the seat next to Owen.

Owen watched her eyes linger on Taylor's exquisite face, then Owen whispered, "She wants to know if she could feed us now."

"Oh, yes. That'd be fine." Taylor refastened his seatbelt and set his tray table down.

The woman nodded and left.

Owen said softly, "I wonder where she thinks we were."

"Giving each other head in the head."

Meeting Taylor's eyes, seeing his humor, Owen began laughing. "Christ, you are something else, you know that?"

"Yeah? You like me?" Taylor reached under the trays for a touch of Owen's hand.

Staring at that brilliant smile, Owen wondered how someone could not like this adorable creature.

Before Owen could reply, two plastic trays were set down on their tables. "Can I get you anything else to drink?"

"Yes." Owen went for his wallet, gave her two fives, and said, "A beer for Mr. Madison, and how about another bottle of white wine for me?"

"Coming up."

When she left, Taylor began opening his foil tray top. "You remembered my last name. I'm impressed."

"It's one thing I pride myself in. My memory."

"I suck. Particularly with names."

Owen finished folding back the foil from his hot meal and replied, "You forget mine already?" He smiled. "I just had oral sex with 'what's his name'?"

Stifling a roaring laugh, Taylor wiped at his eyes, taking the plastic utensils out of the wrapper. "What's his name? Yeah, that's it. Man, you are hilarious."

Owen paused, twisted in his seat and asked, "Okay, then, Mr. Taylor Madison. What's my damn name?"

"Uh, Max? Wilbur?"

"Come on," Owen chided, sniffing at his food curiously.

"It's Owen. Okay? Owen. I don't remember your last name, though. Sorry."

"Braydon." Owen tasted the chicken.

"Braydon, right." Taylor nibbled the meal, then shrugged. "It's not bad."

"No. United has decent food. It's the airline I usually use." Owen began devouring the tiny meal.

The hostess brought them their drinks. Trying to fit them onto the trays, they managed to get everything in place, continuing to eat.

Owen raised his plastic glass up to a toast, "To my first gay experience."

Taylor elevated his beer. "And your last?"

That made Owen smile. "Oh, no. This is just the beginning."

"Really?" Taylor drank his beer from his bottle. "Going to start frequenting the gay scene now?"

Scowling, Owen shook his head. "Uh no. I don't think that's my style."

"Then what? You expect Mr. Right to come up to your front door?"

Finishing eating his carrots and peas, Owen thought hard

about that line. He knew Taylor had more experience on that front, and well, you had to be active to get dates and find a mate, didn't you? Even if you were a heterosexual. Owen didn't answer, chewing on his roll and sipping his wine as he pondered that sad point.

~

Taylor felt badly for bursting Owen's bubble, but he knew better than most how challenging it was to find a decent partner. Men were men, after all. They had high sex drives, they cheated, they loved a good battle, and they hated commitment. Not all, but most. Gay men being no exception. "Look, sorry, Owen. You'll meet someone. I didn't mean it the way it came out."

Continuing to eat, Owen seemed to be ignoring the comments. Taylor didn't know him well enough to gauge either way what he was thinking.

~

The food debris removed, the trays pushed upright, Owen relaxed with that open magazine on his lap of gadgets and trinkets while Taylor rested with his seat as far back as it could go, closing his eyes for the last half hour of the trip. Peeking at Taylor's crotch and slender legs, Owen wanted that blanket back over them again, so he could play some more. Wondering if that would be against some protocol of one-time flings, he sat quietly, inventing scenarios in his head, loving his fantasy life. *Let's see…we disembark, Taylor hands me his business card, tells me where he's staying. After Leah is asleep, I drive my rented convertible to that fancy five-star hotel. We meet, strip, and get to see exactly what each other looks like naked. Maybe some soft romantic music will be playing, I don't know, how about some sizzling jazz, or even better, Beth Orton or some other crooning female singer. We sway softly, uh, he kisses my neck. We move to the bed. Uh…shit? What comes after that? Anal sex?*

"You okay?"

Owen blinked and looked over at Taylor who was staring

17

at him with concern.

"Yes. Why?" Owen wondered if Taylor was not only good looking, but clairvoyant as well.

"You seem a little let down. Is it about where you're going? You know, seeing your daughter?"

Leah? Was he supposed to be thinking about Leah? *Bad Owen, bad daddy*! "No. Actually, my daughter and I have come to terms with the visits. During the week we text, send emails, talk on the phone...it's not too bad."

"How old is she?"

"Ten."

"Was the divorce hard on her?"

"Yes. You know how it is. Kids blame themselves." Owen wondered how they got on this topic. He couldn't imagine it was something Taylor would be interested in and knew it was most likely boring him to death.

"Poor thing."

"She's all right. Like I said, she's had a year to get used to it. It's not that bad."

Taylor touched Owen's leg, as if comforting him. Owen had a quick look around them, spreading the fuzzy blue blanket across both their laps. Hearing Taylor's low chuckle, Owen moved his hand under the cover and cupped Taylor's crotch.

"Last feel?" Taylor whispered in his ear seductively.

"I wish it didn't have to be the last. But I know how this kind of shit goes."

Taylor sat up and turned in his chair to face him. "Yeah?"

Blinking curiously, Owen replied, "Yeah, what?"

"Yeah, you don't want this to be the last?"

A tiny flicker of excitement dazzled through Owen's chest. "You...you..."

"Me, me? Yes, me. You want to try and get together somehow?"

Owen's throat tightened. Get together? While he was in Denver visiting his daughter? Leave after she was in bed? Go out at midnight and suffer the inquisition from Jenna?

When Owen didn't answer, Taylor reclined in the seat, looking straight ahead. "I'll be really busy anyway. I have to be back in LA by Monday. Back on the job site."

Nodding, speechless, Owen didn't know what the hell to say or do. How could you make a decision on a relationship and dating when you had only a plane ride to form your opinion on? Not to mention...it was a *GAY* relationship! *GAY!* Was the mild-mannered tax accountant ready for that? "So, you live here in Denver and work in LA?"

"Yes."

"Oh. I do the opposite. I live in LA and visit here on weekends. That's not very compatible for anything, is it?"

Taylor shrugged.

The approaching landing was announced. Tray tables and seat backs moved upright, garbage was being collected, and Owen and Taylor were silent.

It's an on-board fling. A way to pass the time in a very exciting and daring way. It isn't the beginning of a new lifestyle and romance, is it?

~

Taylor wasn't ready for the amount of disappointment he felt. Initially, he just wanted someone to play with through a dull flight. When he met eyes with Owen and found some mutual attraction there, he thought, "Yeah, okay, why not?" But he liked Owen. There was a desire there to move past the surface and get deeper into the guy who lived inside that fit, tall body and dwelled in the soul and mind of Owen Braydon. But if Owen wasn't willing, then that was that.

Landing with a bounce, the plane decelerating quickly, they slowed to a crawl and taxied to the gate. In silence, Taylor couldn't help but sink as he envisioned the long drive home. There would be no one there to greet him at the door. His friends knew he would be back for the weekend then gone again for the week. He did it every time the company had a major construction job anywhere in the States. That's what he got paid for. Going to sites and managing them.

The plane came to a halt and that familiar beep-beep sound alerted everyone it was safe to stand. Taylor did, moving to the aisle and waiting to get off the claustrophobic plane.

~

Owen stood behind Taylor, hoping the luggage would be unloaded quickly and picturing Leah's excitement when she met him in the arrival area. Jenna would bicker with him, whine, complain, but at least he'd have some time with his daughter.

The line finally began moving. As dully as they boarded, they exited the plane. The repetitive "bye-bye" from the hostesses was annoying as Owen drew closer to the ramp. Taylor was in front of him, his strong, long stride making him hard to keep up with. Owen tried to get closer, just to say goodbye, thanks, or something similar, but the body-language Taylor expressed was distant and cold. It was just a stupid fling. That was all.

Meeting up with him again at the conveyer-belt. Owen wanted to tap him on the shoulder, to wish him a good life, to do something. But he didn't have the courage for some reason, and it seemed grossly out of place to thank someone for sex on a plane. No one expected something like that to be anything more than what it was. *Sex on a plane!* You don't have ties, love letters, emails. It was what it was.

But after sharing that intimacy and not even being able to meet eyes and smile, Owen felt sick to his stomach. It did mean something to him. He just thought if he said it did, he'd feel like an idiot. What did he expect from Taylor now that they had done it?

Owen knew all too well the trap of expectations. And after the horrible divorce he'd just suffered, he wasn't going to get caught out like that again.

~

Taylor's small leather bag rolled around the conveyor

belt. He grabbed it, looked back, and didn't see Owen any longer. Sighing sadly, he left through the departure doors to the main terminal. As he passed he noticed a small girl shouting, "Daddy! Daddy!" Watching her leap into Owen's arms, Taylor smiled to himself and made his way to the parking lot.

Chapter Two

The next morning, before anyone else in the house awoke, Owen climbed off the sofa bed in the den, crept to the kitchen, and found the telephone directory. Just as he was flipping through the pages, Leah entered the room. "Whatcha doin', Dad?"

As if he'd been caught with a Playboy magazine, Owen slapped the book closed and smiled. "Nothing important. What would you like to do today, Leah?"

"I don't know." She shrugged, opening the refrigerator.

A minute later Jenna appeared at the doorway in her robe and slippers. Immediately, she pointed to the telephone book. "What's that out for?"

Growing annoyed that he couldn't make a move without the third degree, reaching over Leah's head, Owen set it back on top of the refrigerator and replied, "Nothing."

Jenna stared the pot of coffee and snorted, "Nothing, huh?"

Staring at her uncombed hair, her worn out appearance, Owen wondered how the beautiful bride he had walked down the aisle with had changed into such a frumpy housewife.

Leah sipped a glass of orange juice. Once she placed it down on the table, she asked, "How about the mall, Dad?"

"Shopping?" he moaned. "Why do we always have to go shopping when I come out?" Owen located a Denver Broncos coffee mug he usually used during his stay and put it near the dripping coffee maker.

"I like shopping," Leah whined.

"Just like your mother," Owen said under his breath but knew both of them heard it.

"You want to stay in a hotel?" Jenna warned.

He did. He wanted to stay in a hotel, find Taylor Madison's name in the directory, and screw him all night. It beat the hell out of the lumpy sofa bed he was banished to in a room so tiny he could hear his breathing echoing off the walls. Knowing any answer could bring on a full-scale war, Owen sat down across from his daughter and whispered, "We can go to the mall."

"Cool." She brightened up and finished drinking her juice.

~

Taylor felt exhausted from traveling back and forth to LA for the last few weeks. Living in hotel rooms and eating restaurant food had taken its toll. Checking the clock, seeing it was only nine, he rolled over in his bed and closed his eyes for a few more minutes of shuteye. When the phone rang he grumbled in annoyance, reaching to his nightstand and picked it up. "Hello?"

"Shit. Did I wake you?"

"Hey, Wyatt." Taylor sat up, shifting the pillow behind him against the headboard. "I was awake, but still in bed just being a lazy ass. What's up?"

"I was wondering if you wanted to get together for some racquetball."

Rubbing his face tiredly, Taylor tried to decide if he had the energy.

"You there?" Wyatt asked.

"Yeah. Uh, I've been in LA all week working on a project. I just flew in last night."

"Right. I remember you telling me that. So, are you too tired for a game?"

"No...no, I should go. I've been neglecting my usual workout routine."

"Traveling does that."

Finding some energy, his feet meeting the carpeted floor, Taylor stretched his back and asked, "What time do you want me there at the court?"

"When can you be there?"

Taylor glanced at his clock. "Ten?"

"Okay. I'll call and reserve it. See ya there."

Yawning, Taylor hung up, motivating himself to get in the shower.

An hour later he parked his pick-up truck in the lot of the sport's complex and hopped out carrying his gym bag and racket. Clouds obscured the sun on the cool September day as he made his way inside the building. Showing his pass to the woman at the desk, he waited for her nod and then walked to the locker room. Inside the tiled chamber, voices echoed off the solid cement walls as men laughed and shouted to each other loudly. Finding an available locker, Taylor dropped his bag and began changing his clothing.

"You beat me here?"

As he tugged on his gym shorts, Taylor found Wyatt's smiling face. "I did."

Wyatt opened a locker next to Taylor's and hung his jacket inside it. "So? How was LA? Get to do any sightseeing in Tinsel Town?"

Immediately Taylor thought about his little fling with Owen. There were some bragging rights in there somewhere, but knowing Wyatt was straight, Taylor wondered if he should just keep it to himself. "It was fine. No, I didn't get to sight-see. I was too busy."

"It must suck traveling back and forth every week. I don't envy you. There's nothing glamorous about flying these days."

Taylor nodded as he sat down to tie the laces of his tennis shoes. "I know. It takes it out of me. I imagine doing nothing but sleeping all weekend."

"You're back out again Monday?" Wyatt had finished

dressing and closed the locker door, taking the little key out of the lock to stick in his pocket.

"Yeah. I will be until the project is finished."

"What the hell are you building?"

"A thirty-story office slash retail center."

"Like LA needs another one of those," Wyatt picked up his racket, swinging it for practice.

Standing up, shutting his locker door, Taylor stared for a moment at Wyatt's pleasant features, deciding on just going for it. "I met a guy on the plane." He paused to see what Wyatt's reaction was. It wasn't the first time he had talked about his sex life.

Wyatt paused, then nodded, as if saying, "Go ahead".

Taylor felt his cheeks warm slightly at the memory of Owen's touch. "We messed around on the flight a little."

"Did you?" Wyatt appeared amused. "Are you a member of the Mile High Club now?"

"Not quite." Taylor started walking out of the locker room.

"Too bad. Maybe next time."

Smiling to himself, Taylor found his way to their reserved court, wishing he could join that elite club.

~

The mall bored him senseless. Nothing was worse than walking around an enclosed artificial environment while his daughter pointed to every horrific fashion trend and begged to own it. How a ten year old could be so completely self-absorbed and materialistic boggled his mind. Then again, she was Jenna all over.

"Don't you want to get out in the sunshine?" he implored. "It's so sunny out there."

"It's too cold."

"Too cold? It's not even winter yet. What will you do when it snows?" He dug in his heels as she tried to drag him into yet another accessory shop.

"I stay inside with my friends and play video games. I

don't play in the snow anymore, Dad. I'm ten!"

"Ooh! Ten! Man, you're old." He resisted her yanking. "Why are you taking me into all of these crappy stores?"

"I like them!"

"How many pairs of earrings do you need? You only have two ears, and I already bought you three pairs."

"That's because it was a buy two get the third one free sale!"

How could he argue with that logic? Dragged inch by terrible inch, he was once again subjected to her holding up long gaudy dangle earrings that would make a hooker look tacky and begging him to open his wallet.

~

Showered and back in his jeans and cotton shirt, Taylor packed up his sweaty clothing, feeling refreshed and energetic after the vigorous game. Checking his watch, he asked Wyatt, "You have time for lunch or do you have to get home?"

"Ariana and the girls are waiting. It was all I could do to slip out this morning without a hassle. I promised them I wouldn't miss lunch." Wyatt zipped up his gym bag and picked up his racket. "You want to join us?"

Imagining the warm welcome from Ariana and the cuddles from their children, Taylor accepted. "If I'm not too much of a nuisance."

Giving Taylor a sideways glance, Wyatt replied, "You know that's crap. Ariana and the kids love you." Wyatt removed his cell phone from his pocket.

Smiling as he followed Wyatt out of the locker room, Taylor heard him say, "Hello, darling, we have a guest for lunch…"

Taylor was glad for the company, but wished he could call home and say, "Hello, darling" to a partner of his own.

~

His bags packed and by the front door, Owen checked the time and looked over his shoulder. "Jenna? You almost ready?"

As if she were extremely put out by the effort, she exhaled a loud sigh and found her jacket.

"Look, I'll take a cab." Owen couldn't wait to put that long distance between he and Jenna. Like clockwork, within forty-eight hours they had gotten on each other's nerves.

"No. It's okay. I know Leah wants to see you off."

At that comment, Owen shouted, "Leah?"

Her voice answered from the upper floor, "Coming, Dad!"

The patter of her feet rushing down the carpeted steps followed. Once they were gathered at the front door, Owen opened it and headed to Jenna's Subaru. Buckled in and on their way, Owen twisted around to the backseat and noticed his daughter busy playing with her cyber pet, something he never did understand. "So, when I get home, you want me to call?"

"Yes. And text me all week."

Smiling at the reply, glad he still made some difference in his daughter's life, Owen whispered, "Then you do miss me when I'm gone."

"*Dad!*"

He peeked at Jenna who was ignoring them while she drove. As with every departure from Denver, Owen felt a slight sadness in his mid-section at the separation from Leah, but with it came relief to have his life and privacy back again. Jenna was very demanding, nosy, and consuming in her needs, even after the divorce the henpecking and whining continued. Though he was glad he had Leah, he sometimes wished he'd been able to make a clean break from Jenna and never lay eyes on her again.

~

Packed, Taylor secured the house, loaded his pick-up truck with his luggage, and walked next door to his neighbor's house. Ringing the bell, he waited, checking his watch.

"Hi, Taylor."

"Hello, Ella. I'm off again and I just wanted to let you know."

"Don't worry, dear, I'll keep a good eye on your place and collect your mail."

"You are a sweetheart, you know that?" He smiled adoringly into the older woman's face.

"I just feel so sorry for you to have to travel so much."

"It's just until the project is complete. Then if I'm lucky, the old man will give me a break."

"You need a nice wife to care for you, Taylor. A good-looking man like you shouldn't be single."

"I'm working on it, Ella." He kissed her cheek and before he walked off he asked, "Anything I can bring you from LA?"

"How about George Clooney?"

He burst out laughing at the mischievous look in her eyes. "You got it."

"Goodbye, dear! Have a safe flight!"

Waving, he made his way to his truck and headed to the airport.

~

Jenna idled the car at the departure terminal. Owen hurried to kiss Leah to allow them to leave the area before security raced over to shout at them to move on. The tension at the airports ever since 9-11 was palpable. No one could relax anymore.

Standing on the pavement in front of United Airline's section of the terminal, Owen waved until he couldn't see Leah's face any longer from where she twisted back from her place in the front seat of the car. Gathering his bag, he stood tall and entered the madness of the building, intent on a quick drink before boarding.

~

Taylor stuffed the ticket-stub from the parking lot into his wallet, then grabbed his luggage and jogged to the entrance of the terminal. As he entered he heard the blaring announcements over the PA to keep baggage close, report anything suspicious, and don't act like a terrorist in general. Finding his flight information on a monitor, Taylor removed his e-coupon from his jacket pocket and headed to the counter. After the long arduous line of robotic-like bodies made their way through the rat maze of ropes and poles, he handed his boarding pass and identification to a uniformed employee and then was directed to a counter. Finally free of his bag, boarding pass in hand, he made slow progress through security and this time was patted down, rather seductively, by a male security guard. Slightly startled by the amount of touching he was receiving, he wondered if it was protocol or just a horny man's attempt at groping. The airport security official never met his eyes. Without a word or gesture to inform him if the experience had been a turn on, Taylor assumed he was free to go since he was now being ignored. He noticed his wallet and keys had passed through the x-ray machine and were waiting to be collected. "Geez," he murmured under his breath and stood for a moment to watch the process. When the security guard did the exact same pat-down to the next man, Taylor felt relieved he was not singled out for a "good feel of his privates" and continued on his way.

Under the bright florescent lights and through the mulling, dazed crowd, Taylor wandered the shops to kill some time before he headed to the gate. Though he had been on dozens of flights, airports never ceased to make him feel dizzy with the amount of action that surrounded him. Maybe it was the lighting? Perhaps the sense of apprehension of an impending crash, whatever it was, Taylor felt unease and usually headed straight to the bar.

A pleasant, yet slightly overcrowded drinking establishment drew him inside. Looking over the beer on tap, Taylor took his wallet out of his pocket and waited to get the bartender's attention. Once he had a Guinness in his hand, he scoped out the area for an available seat.

~

Checking the time, Owen figured he'd head to the gate and sit and read the magazine he had purchased. Walking down the long, hollow corridors of the massive international airport, Owen felt slightly lonely and let down. He missed Leah. That once a year visit for two weeks in the summer didn't seem adequate. And the weekends went by so quickly, he was hardly on the ground for forty-eight hours. It felt more like one day with all the traveling to and from the airport. As he worried about his daughter growing up with a part-time father, Owen found his assigned gate and sat down with his *Newsweek*, thumbing through the articles. Life was never easy; he knew that more than most.

~

The beer eased some of his discomfort. Taylor checked his watch, stood up, draped his leather jacket over his arm and began heading to the gate as boarding time drew near. Scuffing his boot heels tiredly as he went, thinking of the long week on the job site ahead, Taylor imagined a long nap on the queen-sized mattress in his hotel. Reading the numbers of the gates as he passed, seeing his was next, Taylor paused and felt his body surge with excitement. "I don't believe it." There, sitting with a magazine on his lap, was the fantastic Owen Braydon. Pausing to admire him before approaching, Taylor licked his lips at how those tight, faded blue denims hugged Owen's legs, how broad his shoulders were in the beige cotton shirt he wore, and ogled his gorgeous profile with that perfectly straight nose. Having an impulsive thought, Taylor spun around and jogged back to the main area of the terminal, hurrying into one of the shops to buy some things he hoped to hell he would use.

~

Finally after sitting for a half hour, Owen heard the attendant announcing the commencement of boarding. He folded his magazine in half, checking his ticket for the seat and zone number. Already feeling tired, he rubbed his rough, unshaven face and imagined a good night's rest before Monday morning arrived and he was back at his desk. His seat row was called over the PA system. Rising out of the chair, grabbing his coat as he went, Owen moved with the rest of the weary travelers to the darkly dressed staff member who inspected the passes. Walking down the gangway once again, going on autopilot since he had done it so many times, Owen showed the stub of his pass to another attendant and was directed to his seat; window, left side, behind the wing. Stuffing his jacket into the overhead compartment and his magazine into the seat pocket in front of him, Owen sat down heavily and stared out at the tarmac and the action on the runways.

What felt like an eternity later, they finally closed the doors and began backing away from the gate as the head attendant made his announcements, which Owen could recite by heart. Once again the flight was sparsely occupied and many open seats remained. Even though he couldn't recline his seat back yet, he tried to stretch out and leaned his pillow and blanket against the side of the plane to close his eyes to nap.

Feeling the force of the take-off, he opened his eyes. As the jet lifted off the ground and the landing gear clunked into place under the fuselage, Owen became impatient for his little bottle of chardonnay and, ultimately, his own bed. When someone sat down next to him, he turned to look, choking in shock. "Taylor?"

"Hello, Mr. Braydon."

"I didn't see you at the gate."

"I know."

Owen loved the devilish look in Taylor's light blue eyes. "Were you hiding from me?"

"I was."

Smiling, very flattered, Owen gestured to Taylor's seat and asked, "What would you do if someone was sitting

31

there?"

"Ask him to move and find another spot."

"Oh?" Owen had to stifle a laugh at that comment. "And what if they didn't move?"

"They'd move. I have my ways." Taylor leaned against Owen's shoulder.

Owen was so thrilled Taylor was with him, he couldn't stop grinning like a madman. "So, uh, how was your weekend?"

"All right. Didn't really do too much. How was yours? You have a good time with your daughter?"

Once they had leveled off and the seatbelt sign had shut off, Owen noticed the drink cart coming their way. "Yes, I suppose. She's at that age where a good time means shopping at the mall."

"Ah." Taylor nodded, looking over at the cart as well.

They both went for their wallets. Owen stayed Taylor's hand and said, "I get the first one this time."

Smiling as if he knew something Owen didn't, Taylor replied, "Yes, you will."

Seeing that naughty expression, Owen had to wait to inquire what Taylor's comment was all about when the stewardess leaned over to place napkins on their tray tables. "What would you like to drink?"

"A beer for Mr. Madison, and I'd like a bottle of chardonnay, please." Owen handed her a ten-dollar bill.

She set their drinks down along with two bags of peanuts before she moved on her way.

Looking over the seat to make sure she wasn't within hearing distance, Owen whispered, "What did you mean, I will? I have a feeling you weren't talking about the drinks."

Taylor shifted around in the tight space, then produced a small plastic bag from his leather jacket pocket and tossed it on Owen's lap under the tray table.

Owen glanced around nervously, then peeked in. "Holy shit!"

Taylor burst into hysterical laughter, trying to bite it back by covering his mouth with his hand.

Immediately, Owen opened his wine bottle and poured a full glass. Taking a gulp, downing most of it, Owen looked over at Taylor's incredibly handsome face. In a hushed voice, he asked, "Did you just buy these?"

"Yeah. The minute I knew you were going to be on the flight. So? What do you say? Wanna join the Mile High Club?"

Mile High Club? Owen thought that sounded vaguely familiar. Where had he heard it before?

As if Taylor could see he was perplexed, he leaned over Owen's shoulder to whisper in his ear, "Getting screwed while on a plane."

Choking in awe, Owen felt the greatest rush of pure adrenalin coursing through his veins. "You...you mean, screw in that tiny bathroom?"

Taylor shrugged, sipping his beer.

Anal sex? Owen kept repeating those two words in his head. A bag containing prophylactics and lubrication sat on his lap. Yes, that was what he had on his lap!

Nudging Owen's arm lightly, Taylor purred, "I did nothing but think about you all weekend long."

Blinking in surprise, Owen twisted to see Taylor's face. "Really? Me?"

"Yes. You."

"Huh." Owen finished his wine in a hurry. Then, slowly, Taylor took that blue blanket out of its plastic wrap. After lifting the arm that separated them and pushing it back into the seat, Taylor spread the flannel out under the two open trays, across both their laps. A moment later, a hot hand rubbed Owen's thigh. Chills coursed over his body. The semi-erection he had when Taylor sat next to him became a full-blown hard-on, throbbing and dying to be stuck somewhere naughty.

Jumping when the stewardess appeared next to them to

collect their empty bottles and glasses, Owen held his breath as Taylor's fingers halted their stroking momentarily. The heat of Taylor's left hand cupping his dick as it had grown hard down the leg of his jeans was driving Owen completely crazy. When the stewardess vanished down the aisle, Taylor continued to fondle Owen's crotch with loving, creative fingers. Wanting him so badly he ached, Owen's hissed between clenched teeth, "Go. I'll meet you there." Owen shoved the bag of items at Taylor.

"Great."

Taylor put his tray table upright, pushed the blanket aside, unbuckled his belt, and took a walk to the back of the plane.

Owen was panting. His chest was rising and falling so rapidly, he felt he would faint. *Okay. Owen Braydon, you are about to consummate your gayness. Are you ready?* Out loud he said, "Yes." Pushing his tray up and clipping it, Owen folded the blanket into a neat square as he waited for the right moment. W*ho screws whom? Did he mean, I screw him first when he said, you will get the first one?* Or he'd get screwed? Did he want a dick up his ass? What the hell would it feel like? Was there enough room for two large men to have sex in that tiny space they called the head?

Purposely stopping his internal dialogue before it caused him to chicken out, Owen inhaled a deep breath, unbuckling his belt like Batman ready to jump out of the Batmobile to solve a crime. As he walked to the tail of the plane, he wondered if the women in uniform knew. They had to have seen something like this before. After all, there was a club. *A Mile High Club*. Were they smirking? Laughing under their breaths? Or getting ready to call the authorities at LAX to arrest the two perverts? Trying not to believe either argument in his head, Owen pretended they knew nothing and found that one occupied toilet.

He tapped the door. Instantly, it opened and a large masculine hand gripped his shirt and dragged him in quickly.

"Déjà vu!" Owen chuckled as he stood nose to nose and knee to knee with Taylor in the tight space. His eyes were drawn to the metal sink. That bag of supplies had been opened. Two wrapped rubbers were torn from the strip and the tube of lube sat at the ready. Instantly he remembered the incredible blowjob from before and shivered in delight.

Taylor whispered, "Owen? I don't want to push you into anything you don't want to do."

Owen snapped back to the present. "You're not asking me to do anything I don't want to do."

"Good."

"Uh. Can I kiss you again?" About to make a disclaimer that he didn't shave because it was the weekend and didn't want to scratch Taylor's face, Owen's jaw was grabbed roughly and his mouth soon had Taylor's attached to it. On contact with Taylor's lips and tongue, Owen melted.

~

Taylor couldn't wait to get his hands on this man again. For two days all Taylor had done was think of Owen, recall the contact with him, and wish he could have another chance at touching him. That amazing tongue, so curious and timid as it explored his mouth, Taylor was so turned on by Owen's scent, demeanor, and looks, he thought he would go mad if he didn't find Owen again. But here he was. In his arms kissing him. Would they go all the way?

~

Owen had to bring himself back from a swoon. The passion he felt for Taylor was unlike anything he could remember experiencing. Maybe there was something to this bi-curiosity on his part. He liked looking at naked men. *So sue me.* But it was the truth. Did he tell anyone? No.

And Taylor was handling him gently, like he was a virgin. Well, in this respect he was. Though Owen would have loved to kiss for the two and a half hour flight, he knew the time was not theirs to dally and that if they were indeed going to mess around, they had to get to it. He parted from the kiss and stared into Taylor's aquamarine eyes. "What do I do?"

Taylor caught his breath from the kissing and asked, "You want to screw me?"

"Yes!" Owen shouted, then covered his mouth. "Yes," he said more softly.

"I mean, first." Taylor stifled another laughing fit.

"Oh. Yes. Or do you want to do me? I don't know. You tell me. I'm new at this game."

"Why don't you do me?" Taylor opened his jeans and yanked them down with his briefs to his ankles, taking one leg completely out of his pants.

If there had been space, Owen would have taken a step back to admire that physique. Perfect, absolutely perfect. "Christ, you have a big dick."

Chuckling to himself, Taylor opened a rubber, and with the tiny rolled up object in his hand he said, "You have to take your pants off, Owen."

"Oh! Right." Owen's hands shook as he opened his button and zipper. Wondering if Taylor would admire his body or just tolerate it, Owen bravely yanked his clothing down to his feet, exactly like Taylor had.

"You fantastic mother-fucker," Taylor whispered.

"Yeah?" Owen looked down at his exposed body.

"Oh, yes..." Taylor slipped the condom onto Owen's cock, massaging lubrication on it.

Just the touch of Taylor's skilled hands was almost enough to make Owen come. Closing his eyes, holding back so he didn't completely embarrass himself by spurting even before he screwed Taylor, Owen waited until Taylor had finished the preparation process.

Like the last time, the head was hissing and making horrific gurgling noises even with the lid closed. In the extremely tight space, Taylor managed to turn around, leaning over that churning piss-hole and spread his legs wide.

Owen stared at Taylor's muscular ass and thighs in awe.

Taylor twisted over his shoulder, asking, "What are you waiting for?"

"Huh?" Owen blinked.

"Fuck me."

Owen felt his body explode with chills at the naughty talk. "You...you mean, stick my dick up your ass?"

"Yes! Owen, we can't stay in here all day."

The plane listed slightly, and Owen prayed it didn't become turbulent and everyone was called back to their seats. Holding his dick with his right hand and Taylor's hip with his left, Owen moved closer until the tip of his cock touched Owen's ass. "Should I just push in?"

"Yes, dear," Taylor said sarcastically.

Owen did. A wash of pleasure cascaded over his body. After the initial shock, he managed to hold onto both of Taylor's hips and developed a rhythm with the plane's soft listing. Staring at Taylor's broad back, his ass, his legs, then the back of his thick dark head of hair, Owen couldn't quite get over that he was in a plane, in the bathroom, with his dick up a man's butt. "Holy shit."

"You okay back there?" Taylor asked, trying to see Owen over his shoulder.

"Yeah. How you doing?"

"Fine. Ah, could you speed it up?"

"Oh! Sorry. I'm just content being connected to you. Man, it's awesome. I mean, wow. What a feeling." Shutting up, knowing he was babbling, Owen closed his eyes and screwed Taylor with more gusto. Instantly, he came. Pushing his hips hard against Taylor's bottom, Owen whimpered at the sensation and didn't want to pull out. "Christ, I could get used to this."

Again, Taylor chuckled softly.

Pulling out, Owen found some paper towels and disposed of the rubber deep inside the trash bin. When Taylor held him, exchanging places, Owen felt his nerves kick in. He watched Taylor slip on the rubber and then coat himself with the gel. "Turn around," Taylor instructed sweetly.

Owen nodded, leaning over that noisy toilet and held on to it for dear life. What on earth was this going to feel like? Was he insane? Would he feel like a woman? Being penetrated? Would if feel like he was at the proctologist? What?

Hands held his hips just as he had done to Taylor. Taylor's soft reassuring voice asked, "You ready?"

"As I can be."

"Tell me to stop if you don't like it."

"Okay." Owen waited. Warmth contacted his ass. Then Taylor entered him. Gasping in surprise, Owen felt something akin to intense pleasure and his dick stood back up at attention.

"You okay?"

"Yes!" Owen shouted, then lowered his voice. "Yes, oh, holy shit...push in...push in!"

He heard that knowing laugh behind him. Owen closed his eyes and couldn't believe the sensation; hot, massaging, hitting some magic spot he'd never even imagined he owned, and the pleasure it created in him was unlike anything he had experienced in all his heterosexual connections. Hearing Taylor's increasing gasps of pleasure was a bonus. When Taylor pushed in deeply, Owen knew he was coming,, the throbbing echoed by his own pulsing cock. When Taylor pulled out, Owen didn't want him to. Twisting around in the minute space, Owen watched Taylor getting rid of the spent condom, washing his hands quickly.

"We've been gone a long time. We should get back to our seats." Taylor pulled up his jeans and zipped them.

Still half naked, Owen wanted to say something profound. Instead, he gripped Taylor's jaw and kissed him with as much passion as he could muster.

When they parted, Taylor breathed, "Wow."

"You are something else, Mr. Madison."

Smiling shyly, Taylor crouched down to help Owen pull

his pants up. When Owen felt him doing it, he yanked them up and fastened them, tucking in his shirt.

"Let me go first," Taylor said.

"Okay."

Opening the door, Taylor looked out, shutting it behind him. Owen stood still a moment, recuperating. He checked around the toilet area to make sure all the items were back in the bag or thrown out. Once that task was done and the bag was in his hand, he looked in the mirror. Maybe he was decent looking. He just never thought he was anything special. Taylor Madison was special. Of that Owen was certain.

~

Sitting in the seat waiting for Owen to return, Taylor was so satisfied physically, he could nap. Wondering how Owen was feeling after his first gay intercourse, Taylor hoped it was an act worth remembering. He really liked Owen, more than he wanted to admit. And the idea that this was going to be just something they did once in a while on their chance meetings onboard slightly let Taylor down. He yearned for a companion. A real partner with whom he could share every part of his life. Not casual sex. He didn't want a nothing relationship.

A warm hand touched his shoulder. Taylor looked up to see Owen's smiling face. Taylor stood and allowed Owen back into his seat. Once Owen had buckled up again, Taylor sat down and did the same. After a moment in which Taylor was reflecting on their act, he felt Owen nudge his arm. Tilting over to hear his whisper, Taylor hoped it would be something encouraging.

"Hey." Owen handed Taylor back the crumpled bag with the condoms and lube in it.

"Hey," Taylor replied, taking it and shoving it into the pocket of his jacket as it lay crushed on the seat behind his back.

"How you feeling?"

"Fantastic. You?" Taylor tried to read Owen's expression.

"On cloud nine."

"Oh?" Taylor felt his insides shiver. "That good?"

"Oh, Taylor..." Owen shook his head as if words couldn't express it.

"So? Are you going to pursue a full-blown homosexual existence now?" When Owen's cheerful smile drooped, Taylor didn't know why. "Did I say something wrong, Owen?"

~

Owen wanted Taylor. He didn't want to pursue anyone else. But what was appropriate gay protocol? Should he just blurt out he was "in-like" with Taylor and needed to only have gay contact from him? Was that something gay men did? Or were they like heterosexual men with women? *Commitment? Bite your tongue! Marriage? I don't want to be institutionalized in the institution of marriage!*

"Look, Taylor..." Owen began, trying to express what he felt deep inside.

Taylor held up his hand. "I get it, Owen. You don't have to say it."

That confused Owen. Get what? Why did this just have to be sex on a plane? It was painful to digest that fact.

The stewardess came over to their row. "Would you like a meal?"

Owen noticed everyone around them had already eaten. In the pit of his stomach he worried that the staff did know what was going on between he and this adorable man next to him. After they nodded their heads, she brought over two trays and set them on their tables. As they ate in silence, Owen felt let down. He wanted to tell Taylor it was the most incredible experience he'd ever had. To tell him he wanted to see him while he was in LA. Maybe Taylor could stay at this place while he worked instead of a hotel. Maybe they could have sex like that every night until Taylor and he had to fly back to Denver Friday night. But the words in his head never made it out of his mouth. Being a slight introvert, Owen had had this problem before. Maybe he fit the stereotypical role of the accountant; meek, hiding behind his computer and numbers while images of Portnoy washed through everyone's brain at the mere mention of his name. That thought repulsed him. He didn't want that reputation and certainly did nothing to encourage it.

Next to him, right there, was the most incredible specimen of male testosterone and masculinity he could visualize. There. Rubbing against his arm as he ate the tiny foil wrapped chicken and vegetable meal. And he was gay. Yes, gay. That masculine stud liked to make love to a man. So? Why couldn't he be like that? What was stopping him from asserting himself and saying, "Hey, handsome, why don't you come up and see me sometime?"

He knew why. Insecurity. Blame it on his mother. Blame it on his father. Or blame it on Jenna. No. Better yet, blame it on himself. He was the ugly duckling in school, picked on, harassed. Had he turned into a beautiful swan?

~

Taylor finished the meal and tried to pile all the wrappings on top of it so it didn't topple off. Owen was so quiet next to him, Taylor wondered if he was having some morning after-style of remorse. Waiting for Owen to finish his food before he spoke, Taylor sat back, reclining the chair, and watched for the attendant so he could flag her down to remove the garbage from his tray table. A thought occurred to Taylor in that moment. Owen must have a girlfriend. It all made sense if he thought of it that way. They never spoke of meeting up, exchanging phone numbers, nothing to connect them on a deeper level. If Owen had a live-in girlfriend, then this was indeed just an on-board fling. Maybe he shouldn't get his hopes up. Expectations were always a trap. It was what it was.

Seeing Owen had finished, Taylor finally got the flight

attendant's attention and she removed the empty food plates. Once they were unburdened with the garbage, Taylor folded the tray table up and watched as Owen took out a *Newsweek* magazine from the seat pocket. Rubbing his face in frustration, Taylor wanted to see him while he was in LA. He just wished Owen would say something to indicate he was available and interested.

It was an odd circumstance, and Taylor thought he was the kind of man who could handle everything. Maybe he'd been too cocky. He didn't know how to handle this.

Chapter Three

Angry, tired, feeling completely frustrated, Owen opened the door connecting the garage to his house and dragged his suitcase to his bedroom. After unlatching it and dumping the contents into the hamper, he sat down on his bed and felt furious with himself.

It happened again. They were quiet. They landed. They walked out of the plane as if they were total strangers and stood at the conveyer-belt for their bags in silence. It was making his head hurt so much he wanted to scream.

"Why?" he shouted into the empty room. "Why didn't you ask him where he was staying? Why didn't you tell him you want to see him more often? Why, Owen? Why?" He shut his mouth at the sound of his own voice. It echoed back in the sterility of his lonely domain.

Falling back on the mattress with a bounce, Owen stared at the light fixture over his bed and felt as if he could cry. "I'm so fucking stupid."

~

Taylor checked into his hotel and finally made it horizontal on the double bed. Lying quietly, replaying the events from the moment he noticed Owen in the waiting area to the time they stood side by side at baggage claim, to his ride in the rental car, to where he was now. Alone.

Somewhere between that "hello" and lack of a "goodbye" there had been an opportunity. It wasn't like him to not verbalize his thoughts and wants. "Oh, Taylor, you must really like this guy if you can't even ask him his goddamn home phone number." It was the fear of that heterosexual side of Owen that terrified him. The information that may contain the name of some knock-out female partner and the knowledge he was cohabitating with her. It would kill him if it were the case. "Why?" he asked himself. "Are you that hung up on the guy to be that devastated if he's not available?"

When he thought about that question, for a long while, he finally said, "Yes."

Anger began to surface through his exhaustion. It was late. He needed to sleep. Early tomorrow morning he was expected to be sharp and on a job site. He checked his watch. It was after ten.

Sitting up, looking around the bland room with its plain furnishings, Taylor stood and moved to a desk and chair that were crammed into the small space. Sitting down, he opened all the drawers until a telephone directory was located. Taking it out, flipping through the pages, he found Owen's name listed. Pausing, deciding on what to do, he used the pen and paper supplied with the hotel's logo on the top, wrote all the pertinent information down, then slapped the book closed and stuffed it back into the drawer with the ever-present Gideon's Bible. "Okay. Now what?" He stared at the number. Looked at the telephone on the desk. Stared back at the number.

"Augh!" he groaned. "You total chicken-shit! Call him!" Coaching himself, trying to find the courage, the only thing stopping him was the threat of a female answering the phone. Throwing the paper down on the desk, Taylor stood up abruptly, and with his temper raging he stormed to the bathroom to shower and try to get some goddamn sleep.

~

The clock was ticking, the house was dark and calm, and Owen was under the blankets with his eyes wide open. Sleep? Was he kidding? Flashes of Taylor's large cock slipping up his butt were making him tingle and shiver. Twisting and turning under the sheets, punching at the pillow in vain, he could not get any rest.

What construction site was Taylor working on? *Gee, there are only a few hundred around LA. No problem.* He laughed at the absurdity. "Why didn't you get his cell phone number, you idiot?" Owen growled. Knowing he had to get up early the next morning, he sat up, threw the covers off and stormed to the medicine cabinet for a sleep aid. Lying there cursing at himself wasn't doing him any good whatsoever.

Chapter Four

Behind his desk in his office downtown, Owen sat in front of his computer screen and typed figures into spreadsheets and calculated finances and tax breaks for his various clients. Behind his desk was a large picture window overlooking LA's skyline. Trying not to be distracted by it, he had to get busy, or he'd spend his whole day staring out at the cranes and concrete foundations of new projects with the intention of driving to each one and searching for the man of his dreams. How insane was that?

Distracted to a fault, Owen prayed, begged the powers that be, that he and Taylor would once again be on the same United flight this Friday night and they could have another hot session in the bathroom.

"I must be absolutely nuts. My entire sex life is in the toilet. How ironic is that? I ask you?" Looking up, making sure no one was walking by his office and could hear him babbling to himself, Owen shook his head to clear the image of Taylor's unbelievable naked lower half and ground his jaw to force himself to calculate dry numbers.

~

"Taylor! Taylor! Hey, Madison, are you awake?"

Snapping out of his trance, Taylor looked up from a blueprint he had in his hand even though he wasn't even reading it and found the foreman shouting at him. "Yes?"

"They need you down there."

"Okay." Taylor rolled up the paperwork and made his way through the rubble and debris to the waiting workmen.

The sun was blazing and warm even though the summer was melding into fall, and the brightness blinded his eyes. Adjusting his yellow hardhat, Taylor met the men who needed him and listened to their query, all the while he kept telling himself that he *would* call Mr. Braydon, *today, after work, no excuses*. If a woman answered, he'd hang up. No big deal.

Handling one crisis and moving to the next, Taylor had to keep remembering he was on a construction site and this was no place to lose concentration and be nailed with some heavy machinery or concrete. If he could get the sensation of Owen's body, scent, and taste out of his mind, then he'd be all right. But that wasn't as easy as it sounded.

~

Eating a sandwich at his desk, Owen felt his mobile phone vibrate and looked down at it. Leah had text him a message. Smiling in delight, he set his food down, then answered her back. "I miss u 2!" Waiting for her to reply, Owen felt slightly sick about her being so far away. But at least they had this communication to share, along with the emails, phone calls, and his weekend visits.

When five o'clock rolled around, Owen closed down his computer program and straightened up his desk. He was self-employed and leased an office in a large complex so he could be easily accessed from downtown LA. Locking his door, pocketing the key, he made his way down to the parking garage to his Lexus. Owen stopped before merging to the street from the garage. On one corner of the intersection directly across from his office there was a huge construction project. On the billboard it advertised both retail and office space. Could it be? That close to his office? What where the chances? "None." Owen hit the gas when there was a break in the traffic, stopping off at the grocery store for some dinner before heading home.

~

Taylor walked through his door of his hotel room, threw

down his key and sat at the desk. He picked up the phone and before he could change his mind he dialed Owen's phone number. It rang. The answering machine picked up. Taylor panicked and hung up. He wasn't prepared for that. He hadn't decided what to say in case he had to leave a message. It had been Owen's voice and on that message Owen didn't say, "Leave a message and *we'll* call you back," he said, "Leave a message and *I'll* call you back." Singular. Not plural. Was that verification he lived alone? Or was that just the way some people made their messages?

"Why am I overanalyzing this?" Taylor scolded himself. "Just leave a fucking message!" He picked up the phone, then set it down. Unable to decide what to say, Taylor headed to the shower to wash off the dirt from the construction site, hoping while he was scrubbing, he would come up with something.

~

Owen came through his door with a bag of groceries. Checking the answering machine, he hit the play button as he made his way to the kitchen to set the bag on the table.

"Hi, it's Jenna. I just wanted to let you know that Leah needs to go to the orthodontist. She may need braces. I wanted to check if your insurance will pay or you will. Call me."

Making a sour face at the tone of his ex's voice, Owen erased it, continuing to put away his food, leaving a frozen dinner out to stick in the microwave.

Once he was out of his suit and tie and in comfortable clothing, the phone rang. Answering it, he sighed in annoyance and said, "I got the message, Jenna. Yes, I think it's covered, but I have to check."

"Can you please let me know?"

He walked with the cordless phone to the kitchen and stuck his dinner into the microwave. "Now? Why the hell do you have to know now?" Trying not to get unreasonably angry, Owen made his way to his file cabinets and began searching for the paperwork as he cursed at her under his breath.

~

It was busy. Taylor kept hitting redial. After ten minutes he gave up, grabbed his key, and headed to the hotel restaurant for dinner. It just didn't make sense to keep trying. It wasn't going to work, and even if it did, he was in Denver and Owen was in LA. What was the fricken point?

~

His microwave food eaten, Owen sat with an empty wine glass in front of him and daydreamed. Having lived in his fantasy world since he was a young child, Owen felt he hadn't matured a day past sixteen years old, and didn't want to. Annoying flashbacks of being roughed up by bullies on the school grounds came back to him. He was chubby. He had braces...maybe a pimple or two.

Standing, washing his plate in the sink, Owen headed to his bedroom and opened the closet. On the top shelf he found his old high school yearbook. Bringing it to the den, he thumbed through the pages knowing where his photos were by heart. The chess club, the math club, the computer science club...no, he wasn't Mr. Popularity. Never voted best looking or most likely to succeed, Owen wondered what his ex-classmates would think of him now. He was making a six-figure income, had lost his childhood chubby-cheeks, and even gained some bulk from working out at the gym. Seeing how he looked at sixteen, he cringed and shook his head. "Man, was I a geek."

As if to reassure himself, Owen set the book aside, walked to the bathroom and switched on the light. In the reflection of the mirror he studied his face. His skin was smooth and clear, his brown eyes were framed by long dark lashes, his brown hair was thick and soft, and his teeth were perfectly straight. With more scrutiny than he deserved, he judged himself in that mirror. "I'm not ugly." It was the best he could do.

"Taylor, on the other hand…" Closing his eyes to relive the touch of that man's lips, hands, and cock, Owen imagined Taylor was the high school's prom king, captain of all the sports teams and dating the head cheerleader. Blinking his eyes open again, Owen asked his reflection, "He's using you for sex, Owen. What makes you think you're in his league?"

Chapter Five

The long week passed. Though it seemed like forever, Owen was glad when Friday had come and he was relieved from his office duties for two whole days. Would Taylor be on his flight? Would they hook up again, or would they ignore each other as if the last time was the end of these silly sexual antics and they couldn't possibly keep it up eternally?

His bag checked, his boarding pass in his hand, Owen actually asked the attendant, "Can you tell me if Mr. Taylor Madison is on this flight?"

"No, sir. I can't. There's a privacy law that forbids me to."

Nodding, feeling foolish, Owen thanked her and made his way to the security checkpoint. Worried that he would never bump into Taylor again, Owen slumped over and didn't make eye contact with anyone as he put his wallet, keys, and cell phone in a basket on the conveyer belt and passed through the metal detector.

~

Taylor began his search for Owen the moment he stepped into the terminal. Hating himself for not calling him, knowing he was a complete coward, Taylor promised himself this time he would make that effort, ask for Owen's home information and meet with him during the week. Like a soldier that has a battle plan, Taylor hurried to the check-in desk and set his bag down so it could be stowed in the hold of the airplane. As he showed the woman his ticket and ID, he asked, "Sorry, but could you tell me if Owen Braydon is on this flight?"

She blinked, stared at him curiously, then said as if he were hard of hearing, "No, sir. I can't. There's a privacy law that forbids me to."

He couldn't understand her strange tone or attitude. "Did I say something wrong?"

As if she were unable to prevent it, she replied, "It's just that he was here asking me about you!" Then, realizing she had broken her own rules, she turned bright red and pretended she hadn't said a word, clicking the keys on her keyboard. "Uh...you want the seat next to him?" she whispered, looking around sheepishly to make sure no one heard.

"Yes, please. And I will never tell a soul, promise."

Her expression dissolved into a soft, shy smile. "Here you go, Mr. Madison. Gate fifty-nine, row thirty-seven, seat B."

"You're a doll." He winked at her, took the pass, and raced to the security checkpoint.

~

The latest *Newsweek* in his hand, Owen stuck his change into his pocket and was about to leave the store when someone body-slammed him hard enough for him to drop his magazine. Shocked by the alarming contact, he was about to reach down to retrieve it when the man had already done so. Standing straight, Owen looked directly into the wicked smile of the sex god he had been pining over for a week. "Taylor!"

"Hello, beautiful." Taylor handed him the magazine.

Owen took it, trying to get over the surprise. "I can't tell you how glad I am you're on my flight...wait. You are on my flight, right?" Owen began fumbling for his ticket.

"I am." Taylor stopped him, touching his arm. "I'm even in the seat next to you."

"How did you do that?"

Taylor looked around, grabbed Owen's arm and dragged

him to the men's room, which happened to be nearby. Once inside, Taylor gave the cavernous space a once over and pushed Owen into a stall.

Falling backwards from the manhandling and unsure of what Taylor was trying to accomplish, when Owen found himself straddling his legs over an open toilet, he reached out for the walls of the stall to steady himself. Shutting the door behind him, Taylor went for Owen's lips and gripped the back of Owen's head for a good, sexy, passionate kiss.

On contact, Owen ignited. Throwing the magazine down on the floor, Owen wrapped around Taylor's body and embraced him tightly. That tongue, that glorious masculine tongue was seeking his tonsils it was so aggressive. The taste and scent of Taylor was making Owen's cock so hard it was painful. Losing his breath from his excitement, wondering how many cameras were focused on their necking, since everyone was caught having sex in the men's room of airports lately, Owen parted from that kiss and gasped for air. "Look, Taylor..."

"Don't." Taylor stopped him again.

"Why won't you let me say what I need to say?" Owen tried to keep his voice down but he was exasperated.

"Because I don't want to hear it."

His expression going blank, Owen felt crushed. "But..." he stammered, trying to gesture in secret sign language that he needed him, even if Taylor wouldn't let him say it.

~

Taylor could hear men coming and going around them. Toilets and urinals flushed, voices echoed. If he had to endure Owen telling him how he couldn't get involved because of his girlfriend back in his house in LA, Taylor knew he'd be completely crushed. "We can't stay in here. Let's grab a drink."

Owen agreed, nodding for Taylor to open the stall door.

Wanting one last kiss before he did, Taylor cupped Owen's face and licked at his lips and tongue, causing Owen to groan in longing. Pulling back, seeing Owen's eyes closed and the expression of euphoria on his handsome face, Taylor sighed and opened the door. He didn't care that they both came out of the same cubicle. He'd never see these people again. Making sure Owen was in front of him, Taylor followed Owen out after Owen had picked up his magazine and left the bathroom.

Walking silently side by side, Owen gestured to the same bar they had drank in previously.

Once they had drinks in their hands and were sitting at a table for two with a view of the tarmac and planes, Owen asked, "Why won't you let me talk? Please, Taylor."

Taking a deep swallow of the draft beer, Taylor set his glass down and replied, "Because it'll kill me, Owen."

Owen tilted his head, a perplexed expression on his face.

After another long drink from the beer bottle, Taylor said, "Fine. Okay? Fine. Go ahead. Tell me all about the fricken female you're shacked up with. Go on. Tell me all about how you can't have a male relationship because she'll find out about it. Go ahead. I've been expecting it. Shoot."

Owen appeared stunned. About to top off his wine glass with the miniature bottle he had in his hand, he stopped mid-pour and gaped at Taylor in amazement. "You...you..."

"Me? Me?" Taylor replied in fury. "Yes, me! Remember me? The guy who's nuts about you and knows he can never have you?"

Without realizing it, Owen splashed the wine all over the table. When Owen finally noticed the running spill, he set the bottle down and looked helplessly for something to wipe it up with.

In complete frustration Taylor stood and went to ask the bartender for some napkins.

~

When Taylor had left the table, Owen was so stunned he couldn't believe what he had heard. As the wine ran in a slow stream down the corner of the table, to drip, drip, drip onto the tile floor, Owen tried to believe it. In his head he muttered, "Did he just say, 'The guy who's nuts about you and knows he can never have you'?" *Nuts about me? Taylor is nuts about me?*

Once he returned with a handful of napkins and dabbed at the puddle, Taylor's face was contorted with some inner fury he was obviously dealing with. Owen was almost afraid to ask him to repeat what he had said, sure he had it wrong. No one was nuts about him. Not that way. Not in an I-have-to-have-him-or-I'll-die way. Owen Braydon? The fat kid with braces in school? No. This wasn't happening.

Through all the chaos of the spill and the lack of communication skills between them, an announcement rang out for boarding on United's flight from LA to Denver.

"Shit. We're boarding." Owen guzzled the remainder of his wine.

Taylor picked up the bottle of beer to chug down, and they left with a mess of damp napkins and empty bottles littering the tiny table.

Owen couldn't keep up with Taylor's angry stride. "Taylor...wait, will ya? We'll get there. The gate's not that far." Finally Owen had to actually grab Taylor's elbow to stop his steam-rolling progress and solitary mission to the waiting area at the gate. "Mr. Madison!"

That woke Taylor up. He stopped moving and turned to see Owen's face. It seemed as if what he found there confused him. "What?"

"Why are you doing this?"

"Doing what?"

Owen crossed his arms over his chest. "You're trying to ditch me or something. Christ, should we race to the damn gate? Tag, you're it?"

"I'm not doing that. Come on. We need to get there." Taylor continued their progress but at a slightly more reasonable pace.

Exasperation couldn't describe Owen's feelings. As they

whizzed past other travelers, newspaper stands, waiting areas, Owen wanted to ask him what the hell was going on. Shacked up with a female? What on earth gave Taylor that idea?

Just as they reached the correct gate, the attendant called out their row and zone. Owen was so glad they were seated together he could cry. At least now they had two and a half hours of chatting time, no escape. Standing behind the gorgeous Taylor Madison, Owen couldn't stop ogling Taylor's ass and legs and almost forgot to hand his pass to the overly made-up woman with the dyed red hair. Following that tight set of buns down the aisle of the plane, Owen was mesmerized by the way Taylor moved, his strut, his proud as a gamecock gait that screamed confidence and manhood. *Wow, I want a piece of that again...give it to me, give it to me. I just want to stick my face between your thighs and...*

"You want window or aisle?" came Taylor's dry query.

Owen was sick of the attitude. Rudely, uncharacteristically, he shoved Taylor into their row, which only had two seats in it, and said, "Want to know what I want? Huh? I want you to spurt so hard you scream in ecstasy."

Trying to get over the comment and settled down in the window seat, Taylor blinked at him in surprise. "What did you say?"

Getting comfortable next to him, Owen lowered his voice and replied, "What girlfriend? When did I give you the idea I had a girlfriend? I have an ex-wife and a daughter in Denver. I didn't lie about it. I told you." Pausing, Owen then added, "Our feng shui is off."

"What?" Taylor laughed and his brows furrowed in confusion.

"Get up. I'm supposed to sit by the window." Owen stood in the aisle and waited.

~

Laughing the entire time, Taylor climbed out, changed places with Owen then sat on the aisle seat and stared at him.

"You are adorable. I can't get over you."

"Me?" Owen pressed his hand to his chest. "You must mean some other guy, Taylor, because I'm not adorable. I'm insane."

Pushing the arm rest between them up and out of the way, Taylor knew he had time as the boarding process continued before he had to buckle up and sit straight. Twisting as much as he could in the cramped space, Taylor leaned his arm over the headrest behind Owen and gazed at him wistfully. "How can a man who looks as good as you do, say you aren't adorable? You have any idea how much you turn me on? I'm fucking hard as a brick. Look."

Owen's eyes shifted downward.

"See?" Taylor whispered.

"You have any idea how much I want to suck that enormous dick of yours?"

Bursting out laughing, Taylor noticed a straight-laced businessman who was sitting behind them staring, as if he had overheard their conversation. "What are you looking at?" Taylor snarled. The man turned away.

"Be nice, Mr. Madison," Owen admonished.

"Fuck him. So, you don't have a girlfriend?" Taylor asked in excitement.

"No. You kidding me? One child, one alimony check, that's all I need. I have no interest in dating again."

"Er, including men?"

After looking around again first, Owen lowered his voice to a hushed whisper. "You see? That comment screws my head up. Men. You make it sound plural. Well, the word 'men' is plural. Look, Taylor, I don't want to all of a sudden go around spreading my sperm to millions of strange men."

Taylor covered his mouth to prevent a moment of hilarity and then focused back on Owen's words.

Owen continued after another paranoid glance at his surroundings. "I have no interest in delving into gay bars. I'm not exactly Mr. Disco, or whatever they call it nowadays. I'm past all that. I like the idea of a cozy home, quiet, a nice meal out on occasion..."

"I get it." It was Taylor's ideal life as well.

"So, this notion you have that now that I've had a cock up my ass I want millions of male penises to follow, is pretty revolting."

"Did I say that?" Taylor found the same businessman peering over at them, obviously listening to every word. "You mind?" The man once again turned around.

Owen paused, then replied, "You sort of did. You said something like, now that I've experienced gay sex am I going to go out and be...well, gay."

Taylor did recall saying something like that. "I didn't know how you felt. Look, Owen, just because I fell head over heels for you—"

"You...you..."

Taylor stared at him. "You're stammering again. You, you...what the hell does it mean when you do that?"

Owen bit his lip and went beet red.

"Yes!" Taylor tried not to shout, "I adore you, you sexy fucker. You think I want us to just have sex once in a while on the off chance we get on the same damn flight?"

"But...but..."

"But, but?" Taylor laughed in amazement. "But what?"

"But we live in different states."

Taylor's smile dropped. An announcement was made to buckle the seatbelts and put the seat backs in upright positions as they were about to taxi around. Obeying the command, Taylor sat facing forward and put the armrest back down between them, fastening the safety belt. After a minute to think, Taylor responded, "I'm in LA all week."

"Yes." Owen nodded, as if acknowledging it.

"The project has a long way to go towards completion."

"Okay." Again Owen nodded, pushing his *Newsweek* deeper into the pocket in front of him.

"So, let's just say I can see you in the evenings while I'm

in LA. How does that sound?"

"Uh…do you have to stay at a hotel?"

Taylor spun around to see Owen's face. "Is that an invitation to stay at your place?"

"Duh!" Owen shook his head at the absurdity.

"I accept!" Taylor felt his stomach flip in excitement. "You sure? I mean, two bouts of man on man sex in a plane does not a relationship make." Again he caught that curious businessman gaping. "Don't you have anything better to do, mister?"

Owen nudged Taylor in the arm.

"I can't help it. He's eavesdropping and making faces at me as if I'm disgusting him." Taylor snorted in defensiveness.

"Probably wants you to suck his fat cock."

Taylor broke up with laughter and said, "I adore you, you know that?"

"Stop. You'll swell my head and give me false hopes."

As they crawled yard by yard to the runway and announcements were made by the captain about destination, weather, blah, blah, blah, Taylor gripped Owen's hand tightly and asked, "Why do you think I'm kidding you? I mean every word I've said."

"Look, Taylor, you're too good looking to hang out with a guy like me."

That shocked Taylor. "Geez, Owen. You own a fucking mirror?"

Owen's cheeks went crimson.

"You're incredible. I can't wait to see you naked." Taylor looked back at the businessman and enunciated for him, "I said, I can't wait to see him naked."

Owen choked and looked out of the window in embarrassment.

"Christ, the guy wants a blow by blow account of our conversation." Taylor shook his head in annoyance. "Anyway." He ran his hand over Owen's thigh muscle. "But we're headed in the wrong direction, babe. Denver's my neck of the woods and you'll be with your daughter."

"Yes." Owen nodded, resting his hand on top of Taylor's.

"Can you, uh, can you get away? You know, sneak out after she's asleep, so we can fuck like bunnies at my place?" Taylor noticed Owen looking over at the businessman again. Taylor repeated for the man, "We're going to fuck like bunnies at my place."

"Taylor!" Owen whacked him to shut him up.

The only effect it had was making Taylor burst out laughing.

~

Maybe back in high school Owen would have cared if anyone suspected he was gay. Not now. No one was left to tease him, flush his head down the toilet, or lock him in the gym locker room. Nope. He could be gay Owen Braydon from now on. Hearing Taylor's infectious laughter, Owen joined him until the tears fell from his eyes. It felt good to laugh. He couldn't remember the last time he had laughed so hard.

"Meanwhile, here we are on a plane again," Owen kept giggling between words. "Ya got the lube?"

"No! Shit." Taylor shook his head. "I packed the fucking things. I really didn't expect you'd be on all my flights. Christ, were you on them two weeks ago?"

"I was. I book the same ones back and forth. Why?"

"I just can't believe I didn't see you earlier."

Owen smiled. "Would you have pounced?"

"Oh, yes. Big time." Taylor caressed Owen's cheek with his index finger.

Seeing that businessman staring again, Owen just smiled at him instead of reacting defensively. It was obvious the guy was jealous, after all, look at Taylor. Owen imagined Mr. Pouting businessman had a Mrs. Pouting waiting at home with her Mrs. Completely-impossible-pouting--mother-in-law there to nag him in stereo.

"So?" Owen asked, "Back to fellatio in the head?"

"Head in the head. I like the sound of that." Taylor tore the blanket out of the plastic bag and spread it out over their laps in preparation for some good fun.

The plane accelerated like a rocket, pressing them back against the seats; the nose began to angle to the heavens and the landing gear clunked under them into place. As Taylor's warm hand moved to rest on Owen's thigh, Owen tilted sideways to see Taylor's profile. He looked like a Hollywood icon. Owen just couldn't place which one. "Tell me about your life, Taylor Madison."

A warm smile washed over Taylor's lips. "What do you want to know?"

"Everything."

Taylor chuckled softly. "From the time I pushed through the birth canal on?"

Breaking up with laughter, Owen cupped his hand over Taylor's under the cover and replied, "Yes."

"Oh, I don't know. That's thirty-five years of crap to cover in two and a half hours, and we still need time to fondle each other's privates."

"How about just the highlights?" Owen bit his lip on more hilarity.

"Christ, where do I begin? Can you just ask me some questions or something?"

Owen nodded. "Okay. Were you born in Colorado?"

"No. I was born in Texas."

"Why did you relocate?"

In a deep Texan accent, Taylor said, "They only got two kinds of menfolk in Texas; queers and steers, and I didn't have no horns."

Covering his smile, Owen shook his head. "Never mind. Ah, I take it you got your degree in construction? Architecture? What?"

"Degree?"

"Yeah. College." Owen felt Taylor's fingers spider-crawling towards his crotch.

"Just a stupid associates degree in nothing. I worked with my dad to get the job experience. He owns the construction company I work for."

"No shit?"

"No shit!" Taylor imitated Owen's inflection.

"Must be a rich son of a gun." Owen spread his legs in a wide straddle as Taylor began massaging the front of his zipper.

"Yup. Rich son of a bitch. Lives on a sprawling ranch near Houston. Can't say I like the bastard, but he was good for a job."

"Nice."

"I'll tell you what's nice. This fucking cock I'm holding...oh, baby!"

"How come you don't have a strong Texas accent? I only hear a slight one."

"I do if ya get me drunk enough. I learned to *enunciate* my words and not sound like a fricken oil-monger. No one likes a cocky Texan. Most of all me." Taylor closed his eyes and inhaled a breath through his teeth in exaggeration. "Oh, I like that wonderful mound between your legs. Man!"

Owen leaned up in his chair to have a look around as Taylor grew slightly louder. They had finally leveled off and the flight attendants were getting the drink cart ready as a video played a safety demonstration. "You're making me crazy," Owen whispered through the side of his mouth.

"That's the idea."

"I heard it then."

"Heard what?"

"Your Texas accent." Owen shivered as Taylor's hand tucked deeply between his legs.

"Damn! I hate it when that happens. I'm a closet-Texan. Come to the bathroom. They shut off the seatbelt sign."

"Now? Before the drink cart comes?" Owen looked back at the pouty businessman in paranoia. Before Owen could blink, Taylor had stood up and was moving down the aisle. Swallowing his nerve, Owen knew it was going to seem odd for them both to be gone when the cart showed up. "Oh, well." He slid out to the aisle and made his way back to the only occupied bathroom.

When the door opened and Taylor's hand reached out for him, Owen was once again dragged into the miniature space by his shirt. Again face to face, literally, Owen whispered, "I bet that fat guy tells on us."

"How can they prove anything? Screw them. Maybe you're handicapped and you need help taking a pee." Taylor unzipped Owen's jeans. "I have been thinking of this all week."

"Have you?"

"Oh, god, yes."

As Taylor sat on that noisy toilet seat, Owen drew his shirt up, exposing his abdomen and pelvis for him. When Taylor's mouth enveloped him, Owen closed his eyes and shivered visibly. "Oh, Christ, Taylor, that feels so fucking amazing."

Taylor gripped Owen's hips and sucked deep and hard.

A ripple of pleasure washed down Owen's back, then he tensed up his muscles and climaxed, gasping at the sensation. When he was finally able to open his eyes, he found Taylor grinning up at him wickedly.

"Wow."

"Glad you liked it." Taylor stood up and changed places with Owen. Owen buttoned his fly and sat down, reaching for Taylor's exposed cock. This time he was ready. Gripping the base with both hands, Owen went for it with more enthusiasm than his first voyage into the art of the perfect blowjob. It made sense, do unto others what you like done unto you. It wasn't rocket science. Deep, hard sucking, lots of tongue swirling, and a good dose of ball fondling worked magic. The deep guttural moans Taylor emitted as he came sent erotic chills all over Owen's skin. Suddenly, the plane listed and the ride became bumpy. The seatbelt light flashed and a sign read, "Return to your seat."

Owen sat back and exclaimed, "Phew! Just made it!"

Taylor fastened his jeans. "We have to get out."

"Go." Owen nodded to the door.

As they stepped out together, Owen noticed one of the attendants spotted them. Her face grew grim. Ignoring it, he and Taylor slid back into their seats and buckled up.

Pretending he was not going to get thrown off the plane for indecent exposure, bad behavior, or something that the authorities would frown upon, Owen bit his lip and didn't mention the glowering attendant to Taylor. The cart stopped at their row. As Taylor asked for their usual drinks, Owen forced himself to look at the woman. Pinched didn't begin to describe her expression. She wanted to scold them. Owen could read it in her face. Like a school teacher about to shake her finger at them for rough-housing on school premises, she appeared completely irritated by them. Her hair in a bun, looking every part of the schoolmarm, she didn't smile sweetly or thank them for the money as did all the other nice women before her. When she walked away, Owen whispered, "She knows."

"She don't know shit. What can she prove?" Taylor sipped his beer.

"We both came out of the bathroom together. What if she calls some cop at the Denver airport and they meet us at the gate and arrest us?"

Twisting in his seat to face him, Taylor asked, "You for real?"

"Huh?" Owen thought he was.

"With all the damn terrorists and mental patients to deal with, you think some stewardess is going to ask a cop to arrest us? Owen, stop being paranoid."

Was he? Owen sipped his white wine as he considered the possibility he may be overreacting.

"You know how many people screw in the damn

bathrooms of airplanes?"

Gaping at Taylor, Owen shook his head. "No. How many? Is this like a knock-knock joke? Or is it like, how many blondes does it take to screw in a light bulb? Does your question have a punch line?"

After staring at him for a moment, Taylor broke up laughing again, so hard, he had to set his beer down so he wouldn't spill it.

Owen was glad his wit wasn't lost on this incredible stud.

Once Taylor had controlled his hilarity, he asked, "So, how many blondes does it take to screw in a light bulb?"

"One. She stands on a ladder and waits for the world to revolve around her." As Taylor cracked up, Owen smiled adoringly at him. Pouty businessman looked over the seatback at them. Owen asked the man, "Wanna hear a blonde joke?"

Taylor nudged Owen to not talk to the man. "He didn't hear you anyway. He just listens to me when I talk dirty."

"Okay. Seriously now..." Owen refilled his glass with the remainder of his little wine bottle. "So, you live in Denver."

"Check."

"And you want me to try and sneak out when I'm with my daughter."

"Check, again."

"I can't." Owen exhaled deeply. "I want to, Taylor, but I can't do it. First of all, I'm sleeping on my ex-wife's fricken sofa, and it would kill Leah if she found out I had gone off in the night. Logistically, it just won't work. I can't risk hurting Leah's feelings."

"I understand."

~

Taylor took another swallow of his beer, stretching out in the tight space. He wanted Owen with him at his place, but certainly knew Owen's obligations as a dad had to come first.

"Taylor?"

"Yeah?" He stared at Owen.

"You angry?"

"Hell no. Look, Owen, you've got a life, a kid, an ex, I'm not going to cause you any more grief than you already have."

"You're a saint."

"Oh, yeah, that's me. Saint Madison." Taylor knew how unbelievable that statement was. "I can wait. Look, once we're in LA, things will be different."

"Yes. They will. There you can stay as long as you want at my place."

"You have a nice place?" Taylor rested his hand on Owen's thigh.

"It's decent."

"You said you were an accountant? Do they make good money?"

"I suppose some do." Owen sniffed the air and said, "Smells like the chicken again."

"I might try the pasta. What do you think?" Taylor inhaled to catch the cooking aroma.

"Be daring."

"If I was daring, I'd not go back to the bathroom to give you head, Owen."

"Oh, that would go over big." Owen finished his wine and set the glass near the empty bottle on his tray.

Taylor leaned onto Owen's shoulder so he could whisper. "I'd throw that blanket over my head, zip down that fly or yours, pull that prick out of your jeans and suck you like a well paid whore." When Owen shifted in his seat, Taylor smiled wickedly at having gotten a rise out of him. Watching Owen tug at his shirt collar, as if he was heating up, Taylor teased him some more. "I'd stick that long cock of yours so far inside my mouth you'd feel my tonsils. And I wouldn't stop until your hot come was oozing down my throat."

Owen gulped audibly, adjusting his position in the chair.

Taylor felt his own cock throbbing at the sexual talk.

Assuming the narrative was getting Owen in heat, Taylor couldn't resist adding more fuel. "When I get you into a bed, I'm going to ride your ass like a pony."

Clearing his throat, Owen peeked around him again, then in a low voice, he replied, "Crap. I'm hard as a rock again."

"No! Did I get you all excited? I'm such a bad boy."

"Shut up. You knew exactly what you were doing."

Chuckling under his breath, Taylor relaxed in his seat, leisurely finishing his beer. Seeing Owen fussing beside him, Taylor found him spreading out that blue blanket across their laps under the tray tables. Soon after, Owen's hand gripped Taylor's and dragged it to his lap.

With Owen's hard cock under his fingers, Taylor smiled contentedly, massaging that solid mound as he daydreamed of them sleeping together in the same bed.

~

This time, after landing, they didn't behave like strangers. Owen walked with Taylor to the baggage claim area and they waited as the conveyer-belt began moving. "So, I can call you. That's not a problem?" Owen patted his pocket, the one he had placed Taylor's business card in. "But I'll probably wait for everyone to go to sleep. Is that okay?"

"Sure thing. No problem." Taylor leaned around some people to see if his bag was making its way around. "I usually sleep in on the weekends, you know, catching up. I've got a friend, Wyatt, who calls me for a game of racquetball on Saturdays. I'll be up late. Don't you worry."

Owen smiled sweetly at Taylor. "I will call. You know. Just to hear your voice."

"You ol' sentimental fool." Taylor winked at him.

"Yeah. I'm mushy that way."

"You're on the Sunday night flight, right?" Taylor moved closer to the belt as he spotted his luggage.

"Yup. Same one as last week, and the week before..." Owen watched as Taylor grabbed the bag by the handle and swung it to the floor in front of them. After checking the tag,

Taylor said, "I'll wait 'til you get yours."

"You don't have to."

"No. I want to."

Owen leaned over the crowd. "I think I see it. I should just stick it in the overhead compartment, but I hate lugging it around."

"Same as me. Can't stand having it with me the whole time."

Reaching for it, Owen did the same thing as Taylor had, nodding for Taylor to go. "I won't be able to kiss you goodbye," Owen said, his tongue planted in his cheek.

"Be careful. I may surprise you one day and swing you into my arms, dip you like Fred Astaire, and plant one on your lips."

"Wow." Owen wondered how that would go over with his ex-wife and daughter. As they exited the baggage claim to the arrivals, Owen nudged Taylor and said, "There they are."

Nodding, Taylor replied, "So, you calling tonight?"

"Yes. After they're in bed."

"See ya."

"See ya." Owen didn't make eye contact with Taylor when he said goodbye. Seeing Leah already racing towards him, Owen set his bag down and hugged her warmly.

~

Before he changed direction and headed to the parking lot, Taylor stopped to watch the reunion. Assessing Owen's taste in women and seeing how attached Owen's daughter was to him, Taylor wondered why Owen lived so far away from her. Right before Owen left the building, he turned to look Taylor's way. Taylor nodded discreetly and smiled. Waiting until Owen vanished from sight, Taylor made his way to his truck, wishing Owen was coming home with him.

~

After Leah's initial excitement, she sat in the back seat of her mother's car and attended her electronic pet. Owen wondered if it was wrong to want the time to pass quickly so he could call Taylor. "Did you guys eat?"

"We saved you some casserole," Jenna replied.

"Oh. That was nice of you. Thanks."

"Don't they feed you on the plane?"

"They do. But it's a tiny meal. Hardly holds anyone." Owen envisioned Taylor eating his raviolis, offering him a taste from his own fork. "What do you want to do this weekend, Leah?" Owen asked, trying to see her in the back seat as she slouched down and pushed miniature buttons to interact with her pet.

"Uh...I'm having a sleepover Saturday night. Mom said I could."

"Okay." Owen shrugged and caught Jenna's eye as if she expected an argument. "How many girls are invited?"

"Five." Leah rattled off meaningless names, as if Owen was around enough to know them.

"Okay." He nodded again, trying to appear agreeable. "Any special occasion?"

"No. Just a sleepover, Dad."

Under his breath, Owen whispered to Jenna, "Five ten year olds?"

"Yeah. She's been to so many, I thought we were due." Jenna exited the highway and slowed down on the ramp towards a traffic light. "They won't sleep a wink, Owen."

Thinking that same thought, Owen wondered how it would affect his phone conversations with Taylor. Deciding it wouldn't change anything, Owen kept quiet for the rest of the drive home.

~

Into the emptiness of his house, Taylor shouted, "Honey, I'm home!" as a joke to himself. There was no honey in his home. "But that don't mean there isn't going to be one someday," Taylor said cheerfully. Unpacking his bag, feeling the weariness from a long week beginning to take its toll, Taylor stripped for the shower, then relaxed on his recliner, watching some television before the phone call from Owen. It was the highlight of his night. For a change, Taylor couldn't wait for Monday to come so he could stay at Owen's house all week. Then he could shout, "Honey, I'm home!" and get an answer.

~

Watching the clock, yawning, trying to hint to Jenna he was tired, Owen finally said, "Jenna, I need to go to bed. Can you watch television in your bedroom?"

Appearing put-out, as she usually did when things didn't go her way, Jenna used the remote to shut the television off, leaving the room without a goodnight. Shaking his head sadly, wondering as he did with each weekend why he didn't just stay at a hotel, for he could afford it, Owen once again thought of Leah, and the heartbreak it would cause her not to have dear ol' dad in the house with her for the two days. Washing up in the bathroom which was right next to his den and the kitchen, Owen listened carefully for any sound from Jenna that would indicate she was not settled in her own bedroom. Leah had gone to sleep an hour ago, so Owen knew she couldn't hear.

Tiptoeing like a burglar, Owen took the card out of his jeans' pocket and picked up the cordless phone from the kitchen. Moving to the den, Owen shut the door quietly, sitting on his unmade sofa bed, dialing Taylor's number.

"Hello?"

"Hey. It's me."

"Hi, you. Why you whispering?"

"Because I don't want to get caught calling you, duh!" Owen shook his head. "Do you listen to anything I say on the plane, or do you just go blank on me?"

"I listen to you grunt. That's about it."

Smiling to himself, Owen replied, "Yeah, figures."

"You naked? Want to have phone sex? I'm horny as hell thinking about you."

Looking around at the den, the photos of his ex-wife, his ex-in-laws, his daughter, Owen cringed. "Uh...I doubt I can do that."

"I can. Talk me through one. Come on. Say nasty things."

Owen paused to listen. "Are you actually taking off your clothing?"

"Yes. Christ, I'm hard as a brick."

After more rustling, Owen heard Taylor say, "Go on. Say something to turn me on."

Swallowing down his nerves, praying Jenna or especially Leah wouldn't pick up the phone for any reason, Owen almost chickened out.

"Owen? Come on, baby...tell me what you want to do to me once you have me naked and in your bed."

A shiver ran up Owen's spine. "What I would do?" Images of having Taylor in nothing but leather chaps and a cowboy hat, smacking his rump as Taylor rode him bareback flashed through his mind.

"Yeah. Use your imagination."

Visions of leather and whips, police uniforms, playing proctologist and patient, cascaded through Owen's brain until he felt as if he were creating the Village People on porn. "Uh."

"Can't you come up with a thing? Owen, I'm lying here holding my cock."

"Okay. Wait a minute." Owen opened the den door, looked into the dark kitchen, shutting the door again. Sitting down, he cupped the phone and whispered, "You know what I'd do?"

"No, what?" came the eager answer.

"I'd like to tie you up to your bed..."

"Yeah? You would?"

"Yes. I'd tie up your hands and feet. Once you were helpless, I'd play with you."

"How? How would you play with me? Describe it."

Licking his lips, Owen imagined the scene in his mind perfectly. "You'd be completely naked. I'd be in black leather. I'd pour oil all over your chest and make you gleam

71

with it."

"Yeah? What next?"

Owen bit his lip, trying to hear Taylor masturbating. "Uh, after I poured oil on your chest, I'd rub it all over your body. Especially your cock." Owen glanced at the closed door, praying no one picked up a phone extension.

"Good, keep going, Owen."

"When your cock was greased up, I'd jerk your dick like I was milking a cow."

"You'd what?"

"Never mind…uh, I'd…" Owen struggled to find sensual words. "I'd play with you. I'd grope your balls, stick my finger up your ass…then I'd take off my leather pants and slither all over your slick body."

"That's it…that's it…"

Owen paused, listening, wondering if Taylor was getting close. "Then…then I'd sit on your dick and let you hump me…"

"Ah! Ah!"

Owen shut up, waiting. "Ya there?"

"Yeah…I'm there."

Listening to some rustling coming over the line, Owen assumed Taylor was cleaning up the spill.

After a moment, Taylor asked, "Would you really like to do that to me? Or was that just to get my engine revving?"

"Would you let me do things to you?" Owen hadn't even thought of the possibility of anything other than regular sex. If you could call men having sex together *regular*.

"Yes."

Sitting up in surprise, Owen asked again, "You'd let me tie you to a bed?"

"Yes."

"No…no…let me see if I got this right," Owen shook his head and waved his hand even though Taylor could not see his gestures from over the phone.

Interrupting him, Taylor clarified, "Owen Braydon, I will

let you tie me to the bed. What more can I say? Man, you think *I* don't listen."

"I listen," Owen replied. "I listen to you grunt." When it made Taylor laugh, Owen cupped the phone again. "You ever get tied up before?"

"No."

"Huh. But you'd let me do it?"

"Yes! You are thick as a brick, Owen."

"Why me?" Owen looked around the calm room as if he were asking an audience.

"Because. I trust you, for one. Another reason is, I'm really turned on by you."

"Wow." Owen slouched back against the couch and felt his chest swell in pride.

"You want me to walk you through an orgasm, babe?"

"Huh? No. I can't concentrate while I'm here. I'm surrounded by family photos. I told you, I'm in the damn den."

"Okay. It's always on offer, if you want it."

"I want you. Taylor, I can't wait for Sunday night. Our first real night together."

"Me, neither."

"I hope it's all you expect it to be."

"Why do you talk as if I have some unrealistic expectations of you?"

"Because." Owen suddenly felt like a kid back in high school with pimples and braces.

"I'm not even going to entertain this conversation over the phone."

"Okay. Never mind. Look, my daughter is having a slumber party tomorrow night."

"Oh?"

"Yeah, five screaming ten year old girls. Six if you count Leah."

"Sounds like a wild time."

"Sounds like a headache."

"Slip out. Come to my place for some peace."

"I wish I could. No, I can't. Jenna expects me here to keep them in line. The only problem may be our phone call."

"Okay."

"I'll try, Taylor. But I don't want to promise. If they are still up and giggling all night, I might have to pass on calling you."

"I understand. We'll meet at the airport Sunday night."

"Good. Meet me at the check-in desk so we can get our seats together."

"You got it, hot stuff."

Owen smiled. "I'll call you if I can. Tomorrow."

"I understand. Don't stress over it. We've got all next week."

"We do. Goodnight, Taylor."

"Goodnight, sweetheart."

Bursting out laughing, Owen replied, "You are something."

"Yeah. I know. See ya."

"See ya." Owen disconnected it bringing the receiver back to the kitchen to hang on the wall cradle. When he ran into Jenna he died.

"Were you on the phone?" she asked, pouring herself a drink from the refrigerator. "Who were you talking to this late?"

Lies and excuses flooded Owen's brain. Clients, repairmen, business associates, anything but the truth. "Uh."

She waited, wearing her pajamas, sipping her juice. "Owen?"

"Uh..." He looked around the kitchen for an answer to her question.

"I'll just hit redial," she threatened, moving to the cordless.

Grabbing it off the wall, dialing his home number quickly and then hanging up, once Owen finished covering his tracks he sheepishly found her eyes. Jenna was glaring at him.

"Uh…" He couldn't think of a thing to say in his defense.

"Owen," her tone grew more ominous.

"Look, just a friend. Okay? No big deal. Don't start an argument over it. You'll wake Leah."

Setting her juice glass down on the counter, Jenna moved to battle-stance and began her artillery barrage. "I have you stay here on condition, Owen. On the condition that you don't do anything other than visit with Leah. I don't want you calling your floozies or whatever you're doing from my house. You hear me? You keep your personal life back in LA. I don't want any part of it."

"Jenna. It was one phone call."

"Long distance? To LA?"

"No. Local."

"Who the hell do you know local? Do I know her? Is it one of my friends? Owen, it better not be one of my girlfriends."

Cringing, wishing this conversation had never begun, Owen exaggerated his drooping shoulders and dropped his head back, closing his eyes. "Let it go, Jenna. For once, let it go."

As she continued to batter him, not letting a thing go, Owen scuffed to the den, began setting up the lumpy sofa bed, tuning her out.

"You can stay at a hotel from now on, Owen. If you keep sneaking calls to your new girlfriend, you can stay somewhere else."

Pausing in his task, Owen straightened his back and sneered, "You think I like staying here under the same roof as you? Are you joking? I do it for my daughter. I tolerate you."

"Oh, that's it. Get out."

"Get out? Though I can think of nothing I would rather do, Jenna, what about Leah? She's having all her friends over tomorrow night. You want to crush her? Go ahead. I'll let you do the honors while I wait here."

Spinning on her heels, Jenna left him. He heard her

bedroom door close. Sighing, Owen continued making the sofa bed, all the while wishing he could go and sleep at Taylor's.

Chapter Six

Three vacant, oily pizza boxes, five empty bottles of soda pop, and more candy wrappers than a dozen humans could consume at a Halloween party littered the dining room table. Owen shook his head at the sugar and caffeine overload that the ten year olds had ingested and wished he did have a hotel room or, better yet, Taylor's bed to sleep in.

Jenna could shut them out in her upstairs bedroom suite, but Owen was stuck on the ground floor with them. Sleeping bags were lying wall to wall on the carpet in Leah's room, while the girls took turns running up and down the stairs to use the bathroom next to him.

By eleven o'clock Owen was about to shout at the little Indians to be quiet, then reconsidered and wanted them to enjoy themselves. How many times did Leah have a slumber party? Owen couldn't remember one in the past two years.

After fixing his sofa bed up with his blanket and pillows, Owen's eyes grew heavy as *Saturday Night Live's* monologue began. Another sound of pitter-patter and a toilet flushing roused him from his nod. Checking his watch, seeing it was late, Owen moaned and wished he had a sleeping pill. When the noise outside his door subsided, Owen peeked out. The kitchen was dark and he knew Jenna had gone to sleep hours ago, most likely wearing earplugs. Taking that cordless phone from the hook, Owen snuck back to the den, closed the door, licking his top lip, he dialed Taylor's number excitedly, like a little girl at a sleepover party.

"Hello?"

"Hi." Owen loved the sound of his voice. Yes, there was a bit of Texas there, yes indeed. His cowboy. Yum, yum!

"Hello, Mr. Braydon. Are you surviving the slumber party?"

"Could use a stiff one." When Taylor began laughing, Owen clarified, "I meant booze."

"Sure ya did."

"You believe they are still up and giggling? I'm exhausted." Owen checked his watch again, lowering the sound on the television.

"Can't get any shuteye?"

"No. Not at the moment. They keep coming down to use the toilet next to the den where I'm sleeping."

"You are welcome to come here."

Owen groaned in agony. "Oh, Taylor, you have no idea."

"Oh, I do, believe me."

In the pause between comments, Owen enjoyed listening to Taylor's breathing. As usual he spun into a fantasy; *Taylor riding a bronco, coming off all dusty and gritty, leather chaps again, love those leather chaps, gloves, hat, scarf around his neck...*

"You still there?"

"Yes. I have erotic fantasies whenever I think of you. Sorry. Went off on one."

Taylor broke up with laughter. "Soon you won't have to pretend. I'll be in them for real."

"I can't tell you how that makes me feel."

"Try."

Owen smiled so hard his cheeks ached. Another little girl must have drunk too much soda pop, because Owen heard the toilet flush again, then tiny feet leaving the area. "Sorry, someone just came used the bathroom again. Where were we?"

"You were telling me how it makes you feel. Having the opportunity to play out your fantasies with a real live man."

"Was I?" Owen blushed in humiliation even though he was only talking to Taylor on the phone and not seeing his sensual expressions in person. "I don't remember agreeing to that."

"Come on. How much do you want me?"

Loving the seduction, the yearning in Taylor's voice, Owen gave in. "Lots. I want you lots."

"That's it? For all my effort, I get 'lots'? Is that even a damn word?"

Turning to look at the closed den door, Owen whispered, "You know how much I want you, Mr. Madison. I don't have to tell you. If you wait until Sunday night, I can show you."

"You planning on tying me to your bed?"

"Uh, I could. Whatever you want."

"I thought it was whatever you want?" Taylor purred.

"We can flip a coin."

"Oh? Will you let me tie you up?"

Instantly, Owen imagined himself hog-tied by his handsome cowboy, his hands and feet lassoed and sticking up in the air.

"Owen? You must be tired. Why don't you go to sleep?"

"I should try."

"Give yourself a good orgasm. Always works for me."

"There's no lock on the den door. My luck some ten year old little girl will think it's the bathroom and see me playing with myself. Then I'll get sued."

"You sure worry a lot."

"I know. Okay, Taylor. Let me try and get some sleep. See you at the check-in desk tomorrow evening."

"You will. You take care of yourself and make sure no little ones come and snuggle up with you."

"What?" Owen laughed.

"I'd be jealous."

"Silly cowboy."

"Cowboy?" Taylor coughed in sarcasm.

"Fantasy, never mind. Goodnight."

"Goodnight, partner."

Laughing, Owen said, "You are something."

"See ya, babe."

"Bye." Owen disconnected the line. Peeking out to the kitchen, he was about to hang the phone on the hook, last minute, he dialed his own number to erase Taylor's, then set the phone down and returned to the den. The TV off, the lights out, Owen imagined relieving himself sexually, but decided to hold off just in case. By one in the morning, the house finally went quiet, and he fell asleep.

Chapter Seven

Taylor stood near the check-in desk. His bag at his feet, he scanned the moving crowd for his man. He spotted Owen looking rushed, heading to the check-in area. Admiring Owen's physique through his casual, designer clothing, easily imagining him nude and strutting his stuff, Taylor's mouth watered at the sight. Just as with last Sunday night, Owen hadn't shaved. His dark five o'clock shadow made his angular face seem more masculine and rugged. Taylor had to tell himself to calm down. The urge to rush Owen, embrace him, lift him off his feet and swing him around, kissing him passionately was almost too overwhelming to ignore.

Owen found Taylor in the crowd and waved, making his way over to him. "Hey." Owen dug into his jacket pocket for his ticket.

"Hi, good looking. Come here often?" Taylor flirted as they walked to stand in line at the counter.

"Yes. Too often." Owen shook his head.

"You get any sleep?"

"I did. And I grabbed a nap this afternoon. I feel okay."

Taylor gestured for them to move to the woman behind the desk when she called them. Standing together, they handed her their tickets. "Two seats together?" she asked, clicking keys of a computer keyboard.

"Yes," Owen replied, "Window, please?"

"Feng shui," Taylor whispered into Owen's ear.

"Shut up," Owen quipped.

"Here you go," she said as she handed them boarding passes. "Two bags to check?"

"Yes." Owen nodded, placing his, then Taylor's bag on the conveyor-belt.

She tagged them, stapled the stubs to their ticket pouches, then handed them their paperwork. "Enjoy your flight."

"Thanks." Owen nodded his head for Taylor to move on.

Taylor took his pass from Owen, stuffing it into his shirt pocket. "Booze?"

"Booze," Owen agreed.

~

Getting in line for the security checkpoint, Owen waited as Taylor walked through the metal detector, then was stopped and patted down. Watching the young man in uniform rub his hands all over Taylor, Owen swallowed in amazement and imagined doing that to Taylor in public as well. The guard did it, and no one yelled at him.

Owen walked through next, unaccosted, slightly disappointed he didn't rate enough to get that lovely rub down.

~

As they headed to their favorite drinking establishment, the Colorado Sports Bar, Taylor couldn't wait another minute, and dragged Owen with him to the men's room.

"Oh, no," Owen muttered. "What now?"

"I need mouth to mouth resuscitation." Taylor looked around, knew some men were lingering, decided he didn't care, and pushed Owen into a stall.

"Déjà vu!" Owen laughed as he fell back against the rear wall and straddled the toilet bowl. "Did the security guy get your engines revving? Man, he was all over your ass and dick."

"Shut up and get over here." Taylor cupped Owen's rough jaw and brought their lips together. On contact, Taylor swooned at the touch of Owen's tongue. Knowing he could easily get carried away, Taylor wrapped his arms tightly around Owen, pressing their bodies against each other like two magnets, joined at the mouth and hips.

Taylor began humping Owen, rubbing his hard cock against Owen's.

~

Owen could hear several people in the room with them. As water flushed, ran in sinks and urinals, Owen tried to get Taylor under control. A task which took some doing. "Okay...baby...okay," Owen tried to pause their kisses.

"I want to fuck you," Taylor hissed between clenched teeth, slamming his crotch against Owen's.

"We can, all night. I promise." Owen laughed as Taylor's light kisses covered his jaw and neck. "Not here. Too much security in airports now...Taylor, not here."

"I'm no fucking married, republican senator. I can fuck who I please." Taylor wrapped around Owen's waist and pressed hard against Owen's pelvis.

"Really? Isn't your name Kipp Kensington?" Owen laughed, actually loving the aggressive nature of Taylor's advances, not to mention the danger.

"And you're Robin-fucking-Grant." Taylor humped Owen's body harder.

"You read the papers? I'm amazed."

Taylor paused and stared at him. "You think I'm an ignorant hick? Of course I read the fucking papers."

"Then you know that the cops prowl the airport toilets. Let's get a drink and keep horny until we reach my place in LA, okay?" Owen cupped Taylor's face gently.

"Yeah, all right." Taylor kissed Owen one last time, opening the stall door. Instantly Owen heard Taylor ask a stranger, "What the hell are you looking at?"

"Okie dokie, we're going," Owen said, as he grabbed Taylor and dragged him out before they got arrested.

Once they were back on track for the bar, Owen shook

his head at Taylor and said, "You are trouble. Trouble with a capital T."

"Me?" Taylor asked in shock. "What'd I do?"

"Me?" Owen imitated him, "I didn't do nothin'."

"You mocking my Texas accent? I told you I got rid of that accent."

"You didn't, Tex. I hear it more and more." Owen winked at him. "And I love it."

"You love it?"

"Yeah, cowboy."

"Stop calling me a cowboy." Taylor exhaled in exasperation. "I swear when I get you alone, you will be sorry."

"I can't wait." After a long line, Owen finally stood at the bar, asking Taylor, "Guinness?"

"Yes, please."

Nodding, Owen ordered two, trying to broaden his horizons. After all, he'd tried anal sex and that wasn't bad at all.

"You got a Guinness?" Taylor asked when Owen held one in each hand. "I hope you know what you're doing, Mr. Chardonnay." Taylor took one of the glasses from him.

They sat at what was becoming their usual table and Taylor paused before he drank his, saying, "Go on, try it."

Owen licked his lips, sipping the black beer. White foam stayed on his top lip, which he lapped off. "Not bad."

"You're joking."

"No. It's smooth. I thought it would taste like shit."

"Unreal." Taylor drank his. "I hear it tastes better in Ireland."

"We'll have to go and find out."

A look of delight came into Taylor's eyes. "Yes! Travel with me. Holy Christ, Owen, you have no idea how long I've waited for a partner to travel with."

"Yeah?" Owen lit up, sipping more beer.

"Let's plan something. The minute this job is done, I can

take a break. Fuck my dad. He's got to give me some time off."

"We have to go before my tax season starts. So the sooner the better."

"Right, right," Taylor nodded, as if acknowledging it.

"So? Ireland?" Owen asked.

"Yes. Let's do all the U.K. I've never been there."

"I went to England when I was younger. It was with my parents. I didn't have a very good time."

"What were you like as a kid, Owen?" Taylor's eyes had that mischievous twinkle to them that made Owen laugh.

"An ugly freak. Don't ask."

"No way. You?"

"Yeah. I had braces, I was fat...never mind. So, London? Then we'll rent a car and drive to Wales, Ireland, and Scotland?"

"Yes!" Taylor sat up as if he was ready to book the flights right now.

"Okay." Owen sighed. "I can't wait. You're so much damn fun."

"Ditto, my baby, ditto." Taylor took another deep gulp of the beer. "We can hit all the pubs all the way up, make it a pub venture."

"Okay." Owen smiled at Taylor's zeal. "I take it one of us will have to drive on the left-hand side of the road."

"No big deal. I'm not intimidated by that shit."

"Good!" Owen heard their call to board. "That's us." He chugged the rest of his beer and wiped his mouth with the back of his hand, then burped.

Taylor broke up with laughter. "I adore you, I swear, I adore you."

"Finish your beer, cowpoke."

Taylor gave Owen a sly look for the comment, downing the beer in one gulp. Imitating Owen, Taylor wiped his mouth, then belched.

Owen roared in hilarity, falling off the chair and holding

his stomach.

"Come on, Owen. Let's go." Taylor grabbed Owen's arm and began leading them in the right direction.

Owen couldn't believe how strong the beer was. It went right to his head. Trying to appear sober, knowing being drunk could get you banned from the flight, he kept his mouth shut until he and Taylor were seated in their places on the plane. Finally he turned to Taylor and whispered, "Christ, I got one mean head-buzz from that shit."

"Strong, ain't it?"

"Shit yeah. You drunk?"

"No, missy, I ain't drunk. But you sure as hell are. Don't embarrass me, darlin'."

"I won't." Owen looked around the area they were sitting in. "Where's the damn blanket?"

Taylor began laughing again.

Finding the sealed plastic bag, Owen tore off the cover and spread out the blue flannel over both their laps. "Give it to me, come on," Owen urged.

Taylor pushed the arm between them up into the seat, spreading his legs as Owen's fingers walked under cover across Taylor's thigh to his nuts. "We're not even on the runway, and you're already assaulting my penis."

"You love it," Owen hissed, looking around again. Everyone was still busy loading their luggage and finding their seats. "You know what, Mr. Taylor Madison?"

"Yes, Mr. Drunk-Owen Braydon?"

"You have a very big dick."

Taylor choked in shock and looked around. One older woman peered over her shoulder at them, raising an eyebrow in admonishment. After Taylor smiled shyly at her, he whispered through the side of his mouth to Owen, "Remind me not to get you a Guinness before the plane ride again."

"What's your middle name, Taylor Madison?" Owen leaned on Taylor's shoulder, massaging Taylor's cock gently under the blanket.

"If I tell ya, I'll never hear the end of it."

"Come on, please? Mine's Devin, how much worse can it be than that?"

"Worse."

"You let me stick my dick up your butt, but you won't tell me your middle name? How weird is that?"

Taylor cringed, looking at the same woman. She made a "hurmph" sound before she sat down and turned her back on them.

"Tell me." Owen cupped Taylor's crotch tightly.

Taylor jumped at the touch, then sighed. "Austin."

"Austin? Like in Austin, Texas?"

"Yes. Shut up." Taylor shifted in the chair.

"What's wrong with that?" Owen liked the way it sounded. He said it in his head a few times then whispered, "Austin, my cowboy, grrrrr…"

"Sit up. Wait 'til we're airborne to assault me." Taylor eyed the passengers walking passed their seat as they all took a gander at the two of them in curiosity.

"That doesn't sound like the Taylor Austin Madison I know." Owen sat back, moving his hands to his own lap, on top of the blanket.

"I know. Just too many people are staring at us. You know me, I'll pick a fight with one of them." Taylor reached for Owen's hand and squeezed it. "I'm sorry."

Sobering up slightly, Owen said, "No need to be sorry, Taylor. Believe me, right now I respect your judgment, mine's impaired."

"No wine for you, Owen," Taylor warned. "You're driving us home."

"Yes. You're right. I am." Sitting up straight, Owen behaved himself; that is, until Taylor told him to meet him in the bathroom.

~

Taylor woke up after nodding off on Owen's shoulder. Announcements were made for the impending arrival and landing. Shaking his head to clear it, Taylor sat up and put the seatback upright as instructed. Glancing over at Owen, he found him yawning and stretching his back. "I'm telling, ya, Owen, all this sex is making me sleepy."

"Yes, you're right. No more orgasms for you mid-day."

"Shut up." Taylor smiled at him.

After a jerky set down of the plane, the men waited as they taxied to the gate and were finally set free from the confines of the tight seats. After slinging his jacket over his shoulder, Taylor inched down the length of the plane to the stewardess who repeated, "bye-bye" like a skipping record. Once he and Owen were able to walk together in the terminal, Taylor asked, "How far from the airport is your place?"

"About an hour."

Nodding, Taylor tried to imagine what type of house Owen owned. They hadn't discussed anything pertaining to Owen's life back in LA other than his job.

Finally through baggage claim and in the parking garage, Taylor stopped and took notice as Owen chirped the alarm of a gold Lexus. "Nice."

"Thanks." Owen climbed into the driver's seat after stowing both their bags in the trunk.

Once Taylor was buckled in, he asked, "You do all right for yourself, don't you?"

"I can't complain." Owen pulled out of the parking garage and found his ticket to pay the attendant. Once they were on the highway, Owen seemed to relax.

"Do you need a car to get to the job site, Taylor?"

"Shit." Taylor rubbed his face, having forgotten it in the rush to get out of the airport.

"Where's the site located?" Owen asked.

"It's right off Ventura Boulevard."

Owen looked at Taylor strangely.

"What?" Taylor couldn't read his expression.

"Is it the site on the corner of Coldwater Canyon?"

"Yes. How the hell did you know?"

"You don't need a car, Taylor."

"I don't?"

"No. It's across the street from my office. I'll just drive you."

"Are you joking? Your place is right there? You know, I thought about that while I was on the job last week. I swear I was hoping you and I would bump into each other."

Hitting the highway, Owen accelerated quickly. "And I wondered if you were there in that dust pit. It's a strange world, Taylor. A very strange world."

~

Using his garage door opener, Owen paused on his driveway as the door elevated. Once he was parked inside, he climbed out and looked back at Taylor. What did Taylor think? Was he impressed? Or did he have a place back in Denver to rival anything Owen had to offer. After all, Daddy owned a construction company.

Retrieving their luggage from the trunk, Owen hit a button, closing the garage again, entering the house through a door connecting the two. Setting his keys down on the kitchen counter, Owen said, "Come this way. I'll show you where to put your things."

"In your bedroom, I hope," Taylor replied.

Shaking his head, smiling but not answering, Owen led the way to his bedroom. Flipping on lights as he went, he pointed to a walk-in closet. "Use whatever space you need. There should be some hangers in there."

As Taylor opened his bag up and hung some clothing in the closet, Owen stared at him, losing himself on Taylor's body, the way he moved, and the profile of his handsome face. Instantly, Owen's fantasy life kicked in. Though he was about to open his suitcase and empty the contents into the hamper, to set his shaving kit in the bathroom, like he did every Sunday night after his flight, Owen had a different agenda tonight.

~

Mile High

Hanging his business suit in the closet, Taylor was about to turn around and finish emptying his suitcase when he was embraced tightly from behind. "Hello," Taylor said, laughing.

"Hey…uh…wanna get naked and in bed?"

"I see you already decided."

"Yup."

Taylor was allowed to pivot around so he was facing Owen. "You want to shower first?"

"Ooh, yes! I like that idea." Owen released his grip from around Taylor's waist and began taking off his clothing.

Taylor watched Owen stripping off his shirt, then his jeans and briefs. Pausing as he unbuttoned his shirt, Taylor admired Owen's tall, muscular body. Just as Owen was about to disappear into the bathroom, Taylor shouted, "Wait a minute. Get back in here."

Owen poked his head out of the bathroom. "What? I was going to start the shower."

"Get in here. Now." Taylor pointed to the floor in front of him.

Tilting his head curiously, Owen returned to the bedroom. "What's going on?"

"You just stand there until I'm done undressing."

Owen looked down at his own naked body, then up at Taylor. "You mean, you just want to look at me?"

Tossing his shirt on a chair near the bed, Taylor grinned slyly. Next he popped open the button on his jeans, sliding down the zipper, his gaze riveted to Owen's fantastic physique.

Stepping out of his pants and Calvin Klein's, Taylor, now naked as well, nodded for Owen to proceed to the bathroom.

Hesitating, his arms crossed over his chest, Owen shook his head. "My turn to admire you. Wow."

Taylor opened his arms wide and asked, "You like? Is it what you expected?"

"Well, I did see you from the waist down, but the entire package is worth so much more."

Closing the gap between them, Taylor cupped Owen's rough jaw and kissed him. At the touch of their lips, Owen wrapped his arms around Taylor's back and ate at his mouth, sucking at his tongue and lips. Through their kisses, Owen managed to ask, "We're not going to make it as far as the shower, are we?"

"No. We're not." Taylor tightened his hold on Owen, rubbing their cocks together. Moving both his hands down Owen's back, Taylor cupped Owen's bottom and began jamming his hips into Owen's, hungry for some friction and penetration.

~

Owen felt his skin prickle with fire. All he wanted to do was touch Taylor everywhere at once. That was all. Beginning at the top of Taylor's thick head of brown hair and working downward, Owen had the urge to stroke him from tip to toe, then lick him in the same way. He wanted it all. Every inch.

But, he only had two hands and one mouth. Owen did his best to accomplish his need to contact every part of Taylor's body, using his own to rub, thrust, fondle, tickle, and suck where he could. Leaving Taylor's mouth behind, Owen began tasting his way down Taylor's neck. Meanwhile, Taylor had a good grip on Owen's ass cheeks and kept pressing his pelvis harder and harder against Owen's crotch. Finally, Owen let his head fall back, closed his eyes, and savored the hip to hip contact, since it was where all the sensation was emanating from. Opening his mouth to moan in delirium, Owen gripped Taylor's biceps and allowed Taylor to ride him, wanting that cock of Taylor's to be inside, not just rubbing on his outside.

In the middle of his "Aaaaaaaah" sound of euphoria, Owen blinked open his eyes as he was picked up, tossed over a broad shoulder, and carried to his king-sized bed.

Landing on his back on the mattress, Owen stared at Taylor in expectation, both their chests rising and falling rapidly with their excitement.

After a moment when Taylor once again seemed to be admiring his prey, Owen's thighs were pushed wide and Taylor burrowed his face in-between Owen's legs. In reflex, Owen arched his back and clenched his teeth as Taylor sucked on his balls, rolling them in his hot mouth. His legs spread as wide as humanly possible, Owen wondered just how flexible Taylor thought he was. He couldn't actually perform a split, though at the moment he was close enough. Taylor seemed to disappear from view just as Owen felt teeth teasing his scrotum and a tongue lapping at his ass. Shivers rippled all over Owen's skin. He could not get over the sensations Taylor was creating in his body. And the irony was, Owen's cock hadn't even been touched yet. It seemed his balls and ass were the appetizer to the main course. Unable to keep his groans to himself, Owen began vocalizing his pleasure, something he never did with Jenna. His oohs and ahhs were rebounding off the painted walls of his bedroom, as Taylor seemed to be lost to the conscious world and in some dream where Owen's body was laid out like a seven course meal.

Allowing Taylor to lead, to do his thing, Owen felt like his puppet, his play toy, and wanted to be this man's love slave for eternity. It didn't seem to matter that all Owen did was lay there and receive. Owen didn't know if he could move anyway. The stimulation was beyond anything he had ever experienced. It was so aggressive, so masculine.

Taylor surfaced from the deep and commenced with the next item on his menu, the crease in the skin where Owen's thighs met his cock. Long, wet, lapping licks of Taylor's tongue made the goose pimples rise on Owen's arms. Owen's cock was so hard, he imagined it would shatter if a hammer hit it. Had it ever been that hard before? He couldn't recall. He didn't want to recall. All he wanted was for Taylor to keep licking him. How on earth could he compete with this man? How would he please Taylor the way Taylor was pleasing him? He had no idea but couldn't wait to try.

Taylor's tongue found its way to the base of Owen's cock. At the caressing, Owen thought he would come. It felt as if he was ready to. All the signs were there. Taylor's large hands were pushing Owen's thighs apart, even wider. Owen finally bent his knees to prevent the sensation of stretching. Maybe he needed more warming up in the gym before his workout. He had no idea he'd have to be a contortionist. *Forget the stretching, more tongue!*

As Taylor ran the tip of his tongue along the length of Owen's cock, Taylor finally wrapped his fingers around it as well. The heat of that palm, the sensation of being surrounded by skin made Owen flinch with a spasm of pleasure. Instantly, Owen began pumping into that grip. He had to. He couldn't stop himself. Pressing his heels into the bed, Owen thrust his hips up off the mattress in an effort to get that friction. He was so primed he needed to come, and come now.

And the perfect purveyor of oral sex, at the right moment, Taylor opened his mouth and allowed Owen's cock to enter it. That wet, velvety heat put Owen over the edge. With something akin to a convulsion, Owen climaxed and the intensity rocked him to the core. Gasping for breath, his fists were clenched, gripping the bedspread under him. Owen tried to recover. Breathing deeply, feeling that calm, soothing tongue leisurely stroking his cock as he recuperated, Owen couldn't speak at the moment. He was stunned. Completely overwhelmed with the intensity of pleasure his body, with the aid of a superstar in bed, had accomplished.

~

Taylor sat back, wiping his mouth with the back of his hand, and stared at Owen's expression. "You all right?"

"Yes," came the tight word from Owen's throat.

"You gonna live?" Taylor began laughing.

"Holy Christ…"

Smoothing his hand over Owen's solid thigh, Taylor gave him more time to recover, and just admired Owen's body as he lay splayed on the mattress. *What a pretty, pretty man*...He shook his head in awe as he caressed Owen's hot skin. Owen seemed to be catching his breath, slowing his panting. When Owen leaned up on his elbows, he gave Taylor an exaggerated look of amazement.

It made Taylor laugh again. "You're looking at me as if you never came before. And I know you have."

"I swear, Taylor," Owen gasped, "Never like that."

"I take that as a compliment."

"Holy Christ."

"Now I think it's my turn to ride you like I promised." Taylor grinned wickedly.

"You got it, cowboy." Owen rolled over to his stomach.

Taylor hopped off the bed and dug through his toiletries. Bringing a condom and the lubrication with him to the bed, Taylor prepared himself and then paused to get another good eyeful of Owen's body.

Turning around, looking over his shoulder, Owen asked, "You okay?"

"Just admiring the view."

Owen made a laughing noise muffled by the pillows, but Taylor knew Owen felt modest about his looks. Once he ogled Owen's ass long enough, Taylor crawled over the bed to him and hoisted Owen's hips up, so Owen was on his knees instead of flat on the bed. Kneeling behind him, Taylor set his cock on target, then asked, "Okay?"

"Yes!"

Pushing in, Taylor closed his eyes and savored the tightness. After a moment to enjoy the heat, Taylor began moving in and out slowly, deeply, holding Owen's hips to guide himself in. "So, nice...oh, baby, so nice," Taylor crooned.

"Come for me, cowboy," Owen hissed.

A tingle washed over Taylor at the comment. Unable to restrain his need for fast, deep penetration, Taylor quickened the pace and felt it rising in his body, the eruption, the Holy

Grail, the orgasm. Clenching his jaw, Taylor came, pushing against Owen's body tightly. When he could, Taylor opened his eyes and caught his breath.

"Good one?"

Pulling out slowly, Taylor replied, "Oh, yeah. A good one, Owen. A good one."

Owen spun around on the bed, watching him take off the spent rubber.

"I think we're finally ready for that shower now," Taylor said as he took the used condom to the trash in the bathroom.

~

Owen bounded off the bed, following him. When he found Taylor reaching into the shower to turn on the water, Owen hugged him from behind, kissing Taylor's neck. "I'm very glad you're staying here."

"Me, too, Owen."

Releasing him so they could step into the tub, Owen watched as Taylor wet down, loving the way his bronze skin looked when it was glistening. Finding the soft soap and a sponge, Owen began washing Taylor, starting at his shoulders and moving downward.

"You're spoiling me." Taylor's deep voice rumbled in his chest.

"Oh, *contraire*," Owen laughed at the absurdity. "Turn around. Let me do your back."

Taylor spun one hundred and eighty degrees, bracing his hands on the tile. "Man, that feels good."

Owen soaped up Taylor's broad back, ogling his rippling muscles. "Oh, screw it." Owen threw the sponge down into the tub, then wrapped his arms around Taylor's waist and slipped his cock between Taylor's wet thighs.

"Again?" Taylor burst out laughing.

"And again...and again. You got a problem with that, Tex?"

"I will if you call me Tex again."

Owen jammed his hips against Taylor's ass.

Looking over his shoulder, Taylor said, "You know, you can actually stick that in my butt if you want."

"I know. But I'm not going to need it. I'm almost there." Owen felt Taylor tighten up his thigh muscles. It was perfect. There, in the hot rushing spray of water, Owen climaxed, crushing Taylor in his grip, and hearing his own grunts echo off the wet ceramic tile. Managing to lose his breath once again, Owen panted and informed Taylor, "That's the first time I've come in the shower without masturbating."

"Congratulations."

"Thank you." Owen moved back to allow Taylor to turn around and face him. Owen loved the grin on his face.

"Many more."

"It isn't my birthday, Taylor."

"No, but it is like a birth. You're a full-fledged homosexual, Owen. Welcome to the club."

When Taylor reached out for a handshake, Owen cracked up laughing, took his hand and then wrapped around Taylor's neck for a kiss.

~

The alarm set, the house secure and dark, Owen lay in bed with his arms behind his head, staring at the ceiling. Beside him was the most incredible person he had ever met, either male or female, and he was here in his bed. Could life get any better?

chapter Eight

After a quick breakfast of toast and coffee, Owen had his briefcase and his car keys in his hand. Taylor took a last sip from his mug, set the cup in the sink, then nodded he was ready. As Taylor brushed past Owen at the door to the garage, he kissed Owen's lips and said, "That's for looking do damn good in a suit."

"Thanks." Owen shut the door, hitting the button to open the garage up. Once they were seated, Owen started the car and headed out. "I feel bad that I missed Leah's call last night," he said as he backed out of the garage.

"We were in the shower. How were we to know she called?"

"Yeah, but I usually call her when I get home. I completely forgot."

Taylor rubbed Owen's leg warmly. "She'll be all right."

"I wish you could meet her properly. She's a sweet kid, despite all she's been through."

"Maybe someday."

"Do you want kids, Taylor?"

"No. No interest at all."

Owen peeked over at Taylor's profile as he stared out at the passing landscape. "No? No heir to the Madison fortune?"

"Nah. I've got six brothers and sisters, let them take care of an heir."

"Six? Wow. I've got one older sister, that's it."

"Your parents still alive?"

"Yes. They live in Palm Springs."

Taylor nodded.

"You'd like my mom. She's got my sense of humor."

"Oh? I can't imagine that. How could a sweet old woman be sick in the head?"

Seeing Taylor's smirk, Owen didn't take the bait. "Where do you want me to drop you off?"

Taylor leaned closer to the windshield. "Which one's your building?"

"This one." Owen pointed.

"Just park in your usual spot. Jesus, Owen, I can walk across the damn street."

"Just figured I'd ask." Owen entered the underground parking area, pulling into his reserved place. "I can't believe you're working right next to me. I swear, Taylor, sometimes I wonder about fate and a higher power."

"Don't get religious on me." Taylor shut the car door.

"Oh, no. That won't happen." Owen chirped his key-fob alarm, walking to the exit with Taylor. Once they were standing on the sunny corner, Owen said, "Well, just come to my office when you finish."

"Around five?"

"That'll work." When Taylor leaned over and pecked his cheek, Owen felt his stomach flip. *So bold! Two men? Kissing out on the sidewalk? Oh, never mind, it's LA.* Owen waved as Taylor crossed the street with the light, waiting until he couldn't see him any longer, then he entered his office building.

~

Spending most of the day staring out his window to see if he could spot Taylor doing his thing, Owen managed to get a few hours of work done. Last minute he received a phone call from a panicked client about a tax audit. With a phone headset on, Owen typed quickly on the computer keyboard, asking the client questions while he did.

~

Taylor stopped to talk to the receptionist at the main entrance's information desk. "I'm here to see Owen Braydon, the accountant?"

"Okay." She smiled sweetly.

"Sixth floor?" he asked.

"Yes."

Nodding, he pushed the button on the elevator, checking his watch. Riding up to the correct floor, Taylor looked around the names on the office doors for the right one. The floor was crammed with cubicles, all surrounding computers and chairs, now empty for the day. Finding Owen's name on a glass door, and the words "Certified Public Accountant" under them, he rapped lightly first, then opened it. Owen waved him in while talking on the phone.

Closing the door quietly, Taylor had a look around the large, impressive office space, moving to read the degrees and certificates in frames on the walls. A bookcase was full of tax reference books, as well as photos of Owen's daughter. Standing in front of the case, Taylor picked up a tiny picture of Leah in a baseball uniform ready to swing a bat. Smiling at her cherub-like face, Taylor set it back in its spot, moving on to nose around the other objects in the room.

~

"Yes...I wouldn't worry, Barry. Your accounts are all legal. Yes, of course I can. No. Don't worry about that, either. You are allowed those exemptions." Owen split his attention from his call to that incredible tight set of buns wandering around his office. "Yes. No, you can have me there at the time. Yes. I would be happy to. I will. Just let me know when you are scheduled to meet with them." Owen started licking his lips as Taylor crossed the room again, picking up a small knickknack from a shelf. *Oh, yes. Taylor should already be naked from the waist down if I had my way; strolling around this office, his lovely rounded bottom exposed, that large cock dangling down over his heavy balls.* Owen imagined crawling around on his knees, playing tag with him with his mouth and tongue. Taylor would back away teasingly every time Owen drew near enough for a taste. That deep laugh of Taylor's would fill the room at his amusement with the game.

"Yes, Barry. Please don't lose sleep over this. I've done hundreds of audits with my clients. Will you trust me?" Owen made eye contact with the beautiful male stud in his office. Rolling his eyes comically, Owen shook his head to say his client was a putz.

"I've got to go, Barry. Just call me and I'll be there. Yes. Bye." Owen pulled off the headset and tossed it on the desk, brushing his hand back through his hair to fix it if the headset messed it up. "Some people," Owen made a *sheesh* noise as if to emphasize his plight.

"Nice office. Reminds me of something my dad would have given me if I had stayed in Texas."

"Spoiled!" Owen wagged his finger at him, standing up from his desk.

"Yeah, maybe a little," Taylor answered sheepishly.

"Come here, big fella." Owen reached out to him.

When they connected in a hug, Owen felt tingles rushing all over him. "How was your day?"

"All right. The usual." Taylor leaned back to see his face, then kissed him.

Owen closed his eyes and opened his mouth, searching for that tongue. And finding it inside his own mouth, Owen knew if he asked, Taylor would take off his pants and allow Owen his little fantasy. But in reality, they had all night, in a house, alone.

Parting, holding Owen's hips, Taylor smiled dreamily. "I can't get enough of you."

"Christ, Taylor, you make me so horny."

"Let's get home where I can make love to you properly."

When Taylor released him, Owen packed his briefcase, shut down his computer and then his light. He followed

G.A. Hauser

Taylor out of his office and down the hall.

"Your daughter? Leah?"

"Yes?"

"She's a cutie."

"I know." Owen blushed, pushing the down button on the elevator.

"Takes after her dad."

"Aw, golly gee." Owen nudged Taylor.

Once they were standing alone inside the elevator, Taylor whispered, "You tying me to the bed tonight, good lookin'?"

Instantly Owen's cock was at attention and the sweat broke out on his face.

"Huh? Are you?" Taylor leaned against Owen's side.

The door opened and Owen stepped out of the elevator, said goodbye to the receptionist, and headed to the parking garage.

Owen was so excited, it wasn't until he was inside the car with Taylor that he could answer. Finally closed into the compartment, Owen shouted, "Can I?"

"You know you can do anything your heart desires." Taylor took Owen's hand and held it tight.

"Wow." Owen never had anyone say that to him and didn't know what he would do with that powerful a gift. "Even if I said we should bungee jump connected at the hips?"

Taylor blinked at him curiously. "What? Bungee jump?"

"Just kidding." Owen started the car. "Can't stand heights."

"You don't mind planes," Taylor replied.

"That's not the same as jumping from a bridge."

"No. It isn't." Taylor relaxed in the seat as they drove. "And I'm not bungee jumping, not even for you."

"Well, that won't be a problem. Don't worry."

~

Back inside his house, Owen began removing his suit and tie as Taylor stripped off his work clothes to get in the

101

shower. Hearing the water running in the bathroom, Owen finished changing into a pair of jeans and a t-shirt, wondering what they should do for dinner. When the phone rang, Owen picked up the cordless in the kitchen. "Hello?"

"Hi, Daddy."

"Hiya, Leah. Look, I'm so sorry I forgot to call you last night when I got home. Will you forgive me?"

"What happened? Where were you? I called and left a message."

"I know. I didn't see the message light flashing until early this morning, sweetie. I'm so mad at myself. I never forget."

"Mom said it's because you have a girlfriend."

"Look, Leah, even if I do have someone in my life, you come first. It was very wrong of me."

"So, do you? Have a girlfriend?"

Owen's mouth opened to say something. Could a ten year old understand what a gay man was? "Uh…"

"Will I get to meet her? Is she nice?"

"Uh…" Owen's consciousness vanished into his dark gray matter once more. Thoughts bombarded him from all angles; from sitting down in the den in his ex-wife's house in Denver quietly explaining how daddy has a boyfriend, not a girlfriend, to Jenna screaming profanities about not tainting the poor girl's mind at such an impressionable age, to actually inviting Taylor for dinner out with Leah so they could become friends, all the while his little girl was asking, "Dad? Can I meet her?"

"Uh…"

~

Taylor wrapped a towel around his hips. Stepping out of the steamy bathroom, he searched for Owen. Hearing his voice, Taylor approached the kitchen and stood in the doorway when he found him on the telephone. "Should I go?" Taylor pointed back at the bedroom.

"No," Owen whispered quickly, then said into the phone,

"Leah, when I come there this Friday we'll have a chat about it all. Okay? I think it's really hard talking about such an important thing over the phone. Do you understand?"

Immediately, Taylor realized what the conversation was about. Leaving father and daughter to work things out, Taylor returned to the bedroom. He found the rubbers and lubrication, setting them on the nightstand, returning to the bathroom to finish shaving and washing up.

~

"I will. Okay, sweetie? I promise."

"What's her name?"

"Her name?" Owen wished this hadn't happened so fast. "It's Taylor."

"That's a pretty name."

"Yes. Yes, it is, Leah. Okay. Let me go now, and I'll call you tomorrow."

"Okay. Or you can text or email me."

"Okay. I will." Owen hung up and stood to think for a minute. Moving back to the bedroom to talk to Taylor about it, he stopped short when he found Taylor standing naked at the bathroom door. In Taylor's hand was a bottle of baby oil.

"Oh...oh, oh, oh..." Owen felt his insides set on fire.

"I do believe you'll be needin' this."

"Oh my, oh my...Taylor Austin Madison, you are my living fantasy."

"That's the idea." Taylor strut to the bed, set the oil near the rest of the items they needed, then lay back on the bed, spread eagle. "What do you have to tie me up with?"

The sound of Leah's voice blowing out of his head as quickly as if a tornado had hit him, Owen only had eyes and ears for one thing at the moment. A man from Denver who couldn't shake his Texas accent. "Uh, I could find something. You sure you want to do this?"

"Hell yeah!" Taylor shouted.

"Wow!" Owen raced to his dresser and dug around in his drawers. "Rope...rope, string...scarf!" Owen found one of his long winter scarves, tossed it on the bed, then went in search of more things to use.

"Owen."

"Hmm?"

"Owen?"

Owen turned around. "Yes?"

"Forget the ropes. I'll just pretend I'm tied up."

"Oh." Owen felt slightly deflated. "I know you. You'll cheat."

"I will not!" Taylor replied, indignant.

"Will, too!"

"Will not!"

Beginning to laugh, Owen stood over Taylor and shouted, "Will, too!"

Sitting up, grabbing Owen around the waist to drag him down on the bed, Taylor growled, "Shut the fuck up and get over here."

Owen was pinned back to the bed by a very strong man. "Will, too," he chuckled.

Taylor released Owen's wrists, yanking Owen's t-shirt over his head and Owen's jeans down his legs. Once he had stripped Owen of his garments, Taylor grabbed the bottle of baby oil and poured a thin stream of it onto Owen's chest.

"Whose fantasy was this again?" Owen laughed.

"Mine! Yours takes too long. Go buy some rope, Owen, be prepared."

"Yes, sir!" Owen saluted him.

Once a good slathering of oil was pooled on Owen's chest, Taylor set the bottle aside, and with both his hands he began massaging the grease around Owen's torso.

"Nice…I pay a woman good money to do this to me on occasion. Sixty-five bucks an hour." Owen closed his eyes.

"Does she do this?" Taylor used his slick hands to pump Owen's cock a few times.

"No. Should I find out if she will?"

"Wiseass." Taylor sat on Owen's thighs as he continued

to spread oil all over Owen's genitals and abdomen.

"Mmm, that feels so nice. So, let me get this fantasy straight. You're supposed to be the one tied to the bed so I can have my way with you."

"You missed your chance when you began your hunt for the elusive rope." Taylor gripped Owen's cock again, obviously enjoying squeezing it through his slippery palms.

"You keep that up and you'll have sperm in your eye." Owen's body tensed as he began to close in on a climax.

"You think you're that good a shot?" Taylor teased, continuing to pass Owen's cock from palm to slippery palm.

"Wait and see, cowboy." Owen closed his eyes tighter and felt the first sensation of his cock going rock hard and throbbing, pre-climax. Gasping as Taylor dove down on him, Owen shot out come, directly into Taylor's mouth. "Nice catch," Owen laughed, struggling to breathe.

"I wasn't going to miss that one." Taylor sat back, continuing to stroke Owen, but more slowly now that he'd come.

"And I was supposed to coat you in oil. Isn't that ironic?" Owen giggled.

"You still can." Taylor dropped against Owen's chest and slithered around, sharing the grease. "Oh, that feels so wonderful." Taylor moaned, writhing all over Owen's body as if he were an ice-skating rink and Taylor was the Zamboni.

"Christ, that is so awesome," Owen wriggled under him.

"My turn." Taylor held onto Owen tightly, spinning around, taking Owen with him, until Owen was on top.

Sitting up over Taylor's thighs, like Taylor had done to him, Owen found the bottle of oil and dripped it on Taylor's chest. Once enough had been applied, he set the bottle down and saturated his hands with it. Learning from the master, Owen duplicated Taylor's technique of slipping his cock from one slippery palm to the next, until he had a nice rhythm and Taylor began shivering and tensing his muscles.

"You going to catch it, Owen?" Taylor asked

sarcastically.

"You ready to come already?"

"Any minute, darlin'."

"Okay, fire when ready." Owen lowered down to Taylor's waist.

The moment Taylor climaxed, the phone rang. Owen turned his head and was splattered on the cheek and neck. Taylor roared with laughter.

Owen ignored the mess, and with greasy hands, he managed to answer the phone on his nightstand. "Hello?"

"Owen!"

"Yes, Jenna?" Owen sat back down on the bed and tried to wipe his hands on Taylor's legs, getting some of the grease off.

"What on earth did you tell Leah? That you have a girlfriend?"

"Uh, can we talk about this later? Like maybe tomorrow?" Owen looked down at Taylor. Taylor had covered his mouth, seemingly holding back a tidal wave of hilarity.

"No! I want to discuss this now."

"Of course you do," Owen replied, then used his shoulder to hold the phone and wiped his hands on his own legs to rid the slimy oil. *Fuck you, Jenna, fuck you, Jenna.* And just to prove he didn't care about this woman in the least, defiantly, Owen went back to playing with Taylor's cock gently with one hand, caressing it as it softened and relaxed, holding the phone with his other hand. As he spoke to his ex, he found Taylor trying to signal something to him. Owen shook his head. Taylor kept nodding, insisting he look at something. Taylor still had his hand over his mouth, as if Taylor knew if he removed it, he would go into a laughing fit.

Owen touched the place on his cheek that Taylor was pointing to frantically. "Ew," Owen said as he felt sticky goo there.

"What?" Jenna asked. "Ew?"

"Jenna, can I call you back?"

"Owen!"

"Right back. I'll call you right back." Owen hung up, giving Taylor a pained look.

"You missed!" Taylor exploded with laughter. "I told you you would miss."

Standing up off the bed, Owen walked to the bathroom and looked in the mirror. "I've got your spunk on my face!"

"I know. I love it!"

Owen washed it off in the sink, then couldn't help but see the humor. When the phone rang, Owen moaned, "Oh, come on!" Bringing the towel with him to dry his face and hands as he went, Owen sat next to Taylor on the bed and picked up the telephone again, saying, "I said I would call you back, Jenna."

"Owen, what's going on? Do you have Taylor with you?"

Owen gulped and panicked. "What?"

"Leah said your new girlfriend's name is Taylor."

"Oh." Owen's panic subsided slightly. "Look, Jenna, like I said to Leah, this isn't something I want to talk about on the phone. Can't this wait until Friday night?"

"I don't understand you, Owen. What on earth is so difficult about speaking on the phone?"

~

Seeing Owen's stress elevate as the conversation continued, Taylor's humor quickly vanished. Sitting up, rubbing Owen's back in comfort, Taylor knew exactly what was going on and didn't wish that conversation on anyone.

"Jenna, please. I know you normally win our arguments and run over me constantly, but this time I'm going to have to put my foot down. I won't have this conversation over the phone. Period."

Taylor frowned involuntarily. Hating being the cause of any aggravation for Owen, he hung his head and knew all he could do was try and be supportive. That was it.

"No. I mean it, Jenna. Don't call back. No? Fine! Fine!

You want to know why, Jenna? I'm gay, okay? I'm gay, and Taylor is a man!"

Taylor flinched, closing his eyes.

"Yes! Are you happy now?" Owen's voice grew louder. "Oh, no! Go ahead and tell Leah, Jenna. You won't wait for me to. Go ahead. Destroy my daughter's feelings for me. It's what you want to do anyway."

Taylor climbed out of the bed, headed to the bathroom. There, he relieved himself, then looked at himself in the mirror. He'd been there. Taylor had been exactly where Owen was at the moment, but for Taylor it had been with his father. He had to leave Texas. His father said he was sick of the sight of him. At least he gave him the branch office in Denver. It could have been worse. His mother had passed away. So all Taylor had was a strained telephone relationship with his six siblings and a working relationship with his dad.

In the mirror Taylor noticed his blue eyes get watery. He felt miserable for Owen. It had to be worse with a kid. Had to be.

Using a washcloth to wipe off the remaining oil, Taylor heard Owen's voice calming down.

"Yes. Thank you, Jenna. I know it's a lot to ask."

Taylor stood at the doorway of the bathroom staring at Owen as he slumped over, the phone to his ear.

"Yes. I will explain it to her. Yes. Thanks for understanding, Jenna. I will. Okay. Bye." When Owen hung up Taylor entered the room. As he moved around the bed to where Owen sat, Taylor found Owen dabbing at his eyes.

"Oh, baby," Taylor sighed sympathetically.

"I'm okay. She's going to let me tell Leah next weekend."

"That's nice of her." Taylor caressed Owen's hair gently.

"Yes. It's better than I expected. She's usually so spiteful. She was actually pretty cool."

"Good. Look, are you hungry? I can order us a pizza."

"Yes. Okay." Owen stood off the bed and wiped at his

nose.

"Come here," Taylor beckoned. They embraced and rocked gently. "I understand what you're going through, Owen. Honest I do."

"I know. You'll have to tell me about your experiences so we can commiserate." Owen parted from the embrace to see Taylor's face.

"I will. Not now. Go wash up and I'll find dinner for us."

Nodding, Owen headed to the bathroom, then shouted back to Taylor, "Oh, and next time, tell me I have come on my face, you coward!"

"How could you not know?" Taylor yelled back, shaking his head, laughing to himself.

~

Owen cuddled against Taylor in bed. It was warm and snuggly under the soft blankets. Having Taylor was like having a big stuffed teddy bear, only better. Hearing Taylor's breathing deepen as he went under the spell of sleep, Owen tried not to feel any anxiety over Leah and Jenna knowing he was gay. They were loving people, they would support him. Owen could only wonder what his parents would think.

Trying to stop his internal dialogue so he could rest, Owen closed his eyes and inhaled a deep, relaxing breath, concentrating on Taylor's warm body as it intertwined with his. He finally fell asleep.

Chapter Nine

The next afternoon, Owen cleared up his desk and was surprised Taylor hadn't shown up yet. Checking his watch, Owen left his office intent on waiting for Taylor across from his construction site, just in case Taylor had to stay late. When he arrived to stand on the corner, Owen took out his cell phone and dialed Taylor's number, just in case it was going to be a long wait.

"Hello?"

"Mr. Madison. I'm waiting. Where are you?"

"Had an errand to run. I'm back now. Just let me park this rig and get over there."

"Rig?"

"I borrowed a truck. Never mind. Hang on. Are you in your office?"

"No. I'm standing on the corner in front of the parking garage."

"Be there in a sec."

Owen disconnected the phone and aimed his gaze across the street at the high opaque fencing that surrounded the rubble and concrete. A moment later Taylor appeared, strutting confidently. Owen wondered what Taylor had purchased. He was carrying two large shopping bags.

When the light changed and Taylor met him on his side of the street, Taylor pecked Owen's lips in greeting and walked to the garage entrance.

"You going to tell me what you bought?"

"No. Shut up and get in your car."

Using the key fob, Owen unlocked his doors. When he did, Taylor put his packages in the back seat. Once they were on their way home, Owen couldn't resist prying. "Is it a present?"

"No."

"No? Is it new clothing for you?"

"Why are you so damn nosy?" Taylor smiled at him.

"Because I have a very vivid imagination. And if I don't get the information out of you, I'll just invent something outlandish in my head."

"Good. Invent something."

"You are a bastard, Mr. Madison."

"Damn straight." Taylor rubbed Owen's thigh warmly. "Your bastard. Now get us home."

Sensing some wonderful surprise, Owen did indeed begin imagining scenarios in his head, dying of curiosity. Taylor's smile was planted on his face, another reason to suspect him of conspiring.

Parked, the garage shut, Owen waited, watching as Taylor retrieved the bags while he waited for the clue he needed to guess the secret.

Immediately, Taylor left Owen standing in the hall as he hurried to hide whatever it was he had purchased. "Taylor!" Owen hollered in exasperation.

"You stay out! You hear me?"

"Unfair! No secrets!" Owen shouted through the closed door. "Is it rope?"

"Buy your own damn rope!"

"Not rope..." Owen touched his lip, trying to solve the riddle. "I have to change out of my suit, Mr. Madison."

The door opened and a breathless Taylor nodded, "Come in, get changed. But while I'm in the shower you better not go peek."

"Oh, come on. You know I have to," Owen said as he began removing his tie.

"Don't you dare." Taylor waved his finger at him.

"Then it is a surprise." Owen hung up his suit jacket and looked down at the mysterious shopping bags, trying to read the store name.

A large hand reached for Owen's shoulder, dragging him out of the closet. When Owen spun around, he found Taylor's impatient gaze. "Get away from those bags, Owen Braydon."

"I have to hang up my suit." Owen tried to move Taylor out of his way so he could get back into the closet and peek.

"I'm gonna get mad. Now, leave the damn things alone so I can shower."

At his tone, Owen gave in. "Okay. Promise."

Without another word, Taylor entered the bathroom, closing the door.

Owen took off his trousers, staring at the closet. A promise was a promise. Changing into comfy clothing, Owen headed to the kitchen to decide about dinner. After eying the selection of frozen, unappetizing meals, he located a menu for Chinese food and was about to return to the bedroom to ask what Taylor wanted to order. Jiggling the handle, he found his bedroom door locked. "Did you lock me out?"

"Yes! Give me a minute."

"I was going to order some Chinese food. What kind do you like? You want me to read the menu for you?" Owen put his ear to the door but couldn't hear anything. "What the hell are you doing in there?"

The door swung open.

Owen almost fell over from the shock.

There, standing in front of him, wearing nothing but a cowboy hat, boots, and a pair of leather chaps, was his dream man. Speechless, Owen tried to recall if he had told Taylor about his wicked little fantasy and couldn't for the life of him remember.

"You all right?" Taylor asked in concern.

Owen shook his head in awe, the menu falling out of his hand to land silently on the floor.

Taylor tilted down to stare into Owen's face from under the brim of his black hat. "Say something."

"I...I..."

"You...you?" Taylor echoed. "No good? I thought I was on the right track."

"You...you..." Owen stammered, pointing at the chaps and the naked body under them.

"Me, me, what? Owen Braydon, will you say something intelligible? You're stammering like a schoolboy."

That woke Owen up. *School boy? Who you calling a pimple-faced school boy?* Grabbing Taylor around the waist, Owen wrestled him backwards to the bed, throwing him down on the mattress.

"That's more like it!" Taylor exclaimed.

Breathless from excitement, Owen knelt up over him and stared at the whole image Taylor presented. "Taylor, you are a mind-reader."

"Mind-reader? Ya kept calling me cowboy and Tex. Why do you think I am, an idiot?"

"Because no one else has ever anticipated my desires or my needs, like this. I mean, I was married to a woman for fifteen years and she never even knew me well enough to buy me a single thing I wanted as a gift, no matter what hints I gave her," he announced.

"You going to kneel there, talking about your ex and staring at me all day?"

"Talking, no. Staring? Uh huh." Nodding, Owen then suggested, "Gloves. You should be wearing kid gloves. Oh, and I'd tie a bandana around your neck next time."

"Anything else?" Taylor asked in disbelief.

"Uh..." Owen checked him from top to bottom. "Damn! Chaps without jeans under them. Too bad that's not a popular look."

"You ever been to a gay bar?" Taylor asked.

"No. Do they dress like that in them?"

"Close. Are you done talking? You said you were done talking."

"I'm done talking." Owen dropped down between Taylor's legs and nuzzled his face against Taylor's soft genitals. Smoothing each hand over the supple leather chaps covering Taylor's thighs, Owen felt that soft cock becoming hard quickly. Standing, yanking his shirt over his head, dropping his jeans down to the floor, Owen stepped out of his lower half of clothing and found the rubbers and lube. As he stared at Taylor in his amazing get-up, Owen slipped on a rubber and knelt between Taylor's knees. One by one, Owen raised Taylor's legs to rest on his shoulders.

"Oh, Taylor...you were made to wear a cowboy hat." Owen pushed his cock in-between Taylor's legs, penetrating his ass.

"I hate to admit it's not the first one I've owned."

Owen pushed in deeply, using his hands to smooth over Taylor's legs, feeling the black, silver tipped cowboy boots and the chaps as he pumped. His gaze never leaving Taylor's face and that hat, Owen couldn't believe he was actually living out one of his silly daydreams. Almost distracted with the multitude of costumes he could dress this living doll in, Owen had to concentrate on what he was doing, screwing Taylor in chaps.

The sensation coming to a peak, Owen closed his eyes involuntarily and climaxed, throwing back his head and gasping in pleasure. Coming back to reality slowly, Owen opened his eyes and found Taylor's contented grin.

"You look fantastic when you come," Taylor whispered sensually.

Grinning, then laughing at the thought, Owen replied, "I can't imagine looking fantastic. Most likely more like I'm having an epileptic fit."

"Shut up. You do say the stupidest things."

Pulling out, Owen dropped the used condom on the floor,

gazing down between Taylor's legs. Slowly removing Taylor's calves from his shoulders, Owen set them down gently, making himself comfortably between them. Using his cheek, Owen caressed Taylor's cock, smoothing his coarse jaw along Taylor's soft skin. "Too rough for you?"

"No," came a breathless reply.

Wondering if Taylor liked a bit of rough-play, Owen held Taylor's cock still, pressing slightly harder against him, as if he could polish Taylor's penis with his sandpaper five o'clock shadow. Taylor jumped slightly. "Should I stop?" Owen asked.

"No."

"Oh, baby!" Owen was beginning to get the idea Taylor did indeed enjoy some pain mixed with pleasure. Very gently, Owen placed Taylor's cock in his mouth, then as slowly as he could, he used the tips of his teeth, dragging them, ever so lightly against Taylor's skin. Pausing, Owen asked, "Too rough?"

"NO!"

"Yipes! Just asking. I don't want to hurt you."

Lowering his voice, Taylor assured Owen, "If it hurts, I'll let you know."

"Okay. Fair enough."

"I'm kinda liking it. It's something I never tried."

"Oh?" Owen perked up. The thought of giving Taylor a first of anything was hard for him to believe, but he loved the possibility. Once again, he held Taylor's cock firmly and rubbed his jaw against it. Getting into a pattern, Owen roughed him up, then sucked him to soothe him. It seemed to be doing the trick. Taylor's hips were rising off the bed as he arched his back, those new cowboy boots were digging their heels into the mattress. Seeing the skin of Taylor's cock becoming red, Owen let up on the jaw rubbing and used his hand to continue stimulating it. Taylor's legs tensed up. Owen wasn't going to miss this time. Sucking on Taylor's cock, deep, hard, and fast, Owen revved up his hand motion in time with his mouth. As if Taylor elevated off the bed, his body writhed and then Owen tasted come. Closing his eyes as it slid down his throat, Owen savored the lovely throbbing between his lips, then sat back and stared at Taylor.

~

Taylor lay still, trying to recover from the climax. As he did, several thoughts passed through his mind. Did he like it rough? A little pain mixed with pleasure? He must because the sensation of that sand-paper grit of Owen's jaw on his cock had sent shockwaves through him. Intense ones.

Blinking his eyes open, Taylor found Owen's knowing smile.

"You bad, bad boy," Owen teased.

"I, uh," it was Taylor's turn to be speechless.

"You, uh, what?" Owen repeated, just like Taylor always did to him.

"I...I..."

"You, you?" Owen started laughing. "Admit it, you're into S and M!"

"S and M?" Taylor snorted sarcastically. "You even know what S and M is?"

"I think I do." Owen crawled along Taylor's body so he could lie down on top of him. "It's like whips and chains and stuff."

"Yes. You see a whip anywhere?" Taylor wrapped his arms around Owen when they were face to face on the pillows.

Owen reached to remove Taylor's hat, which had fallen partway off during their sexual bout. After he had tossed it on the floor, Owen asked, "You wanted me to tie you to the bed? Sexually torment you? What do you think that's all about?"

"I don't know." Taylor didn't want to admit a thing.

"Bondage, Mr. Madison. Bondage."

"Oh, shut up. You think you're so damn smart." Taylor loved the look of wickedness in Owen's eyes.

"I can spank you."

"Spank me? Give me a break."

"Slap that hard rump of yours...smack, smack..."

"I'll smack, smack you. Now, did you mention Chinese food?"

"Yes."

"Good. I'm starved."

After kissing him, Owen climbed off the bed to get the menu from the floor. "What do you like?"

"Anything. Order what you want. I'll eat it."

Nodding, Owen picked up the phone.

As Taylor watched Owen standing naked in the doorway, ordering their food, he imagined Owen in leather, smacking his bare bottom. "What on earth have I gotten myself into?" Taylor smiled.

Chapter Ten

Wednesday, after Owen had dropped Taylor off, he pretended to enter his office building. The moment Taylor had disappeared into the constructions site, Owen hurried back to his car for his own shopping excursion. Grinning wickedly, Owen hadn't had this much fun since…

Pausing, Owen said, "I've never had this much fun." Giggling like a fiend, he drove to the mall, hoping they had everything he needed.

~

His trunk loaded with the oddest collection of paraphernalia he could ever imagine purchasing, Owen overcame the embarrassment of buying the items, standing tall and proud as if to say, "Yes, I do have an interesting sex life. Ha! So there!"

In the past just buying rubbers was enough to make him shiver in his shorts. Not any longer. The new Owen Braydon was out, confident, and happy at home.

Just as he drove underneath his office building to the garage, his mobile phone made a noise. Parking, Owen checked it and found a text message from Leah. It read, "Can't wait 2 meet T. Bet she's pretty." Wondering if it was perhaps a bad idea to make Jenna wait a week before telling Leah about the gender of his friend, Owen sighed. "You made your bed, Owen, sleep in it." Owen texted her back,

"U'll C soon." Wanting to be honest, hating deceiving her, Owen checked the time of his watch and knew Leah must be texting him from school. It was too early to call her. But he would call her tonight. Tonight. Had to.

~

Taylor stood in the portable office trailer looking over blueprints. Hearing a phone ring, he looked up at one of the secretaries and caught her eye. She cupped the phone and mouthed, "Your dad."

Nodding, Taylor took the cordless phone from her and said, "Ya there?"

"Taylor? How's the job coming?"

"Good. The contractors are top notch."

"When will you be done? I've got one over in Cleveland that needs you."

Taylor felt a twinge of regret knowing when he left LA, the week long bouts of sex would go with it. "Uh, I don't know as of yet. Can't you send Noah over there?"

"He ain't got the same control over the guys as you do. You can't have more than another few days there."

"You kidding me?" Taylor replied, wondering if Owen thought he had that same strong Texas drawl his dad did. Walking to the doorway to look out at the site, Taylor said, "It's just foundations, Pop. I can't leave until I got it up and nearly done. You know what happens when I do. They start falling behind."

"You just get it going right. I'll send Noah there to finish."

"No." Taylor knew what the reaction would be before he said it. But he was not about to miss another few weeks in Owen's bed. Not for his father's whims.

"No? What do you mean no?"

"I want to finish the job I started."

"And I said let Noah finish it, and you go to Cleveland."

Looking over his shoulder at the other employees in the trailer pretending not to listen, Taylor walked outside, cupping the phone to his ear to shut out the noise around him. "Look, Pop, I'm not givin' in on this one. It's a huge project, and I don't feel right leaving in the damn middle."

"You don't have to tell me how important it is! I know how important it is! And the job in Cleveland is just as important. Let Noah finish the goddamn LA job. You got them all on target. They know what's expected of them. He'll just take over and keep an eye."

Taylor felt like screaming. It was sound logic. He'd done it before. Noah would just take over and the guys on the site would think he was as tough a manager as Taylor was. No problem. But this time, there was a problem. A big one.

"Are you there?" his father shouted.

"Yeah. I'm here. Look, Pop, it ain't just the site."

"What then? I've got work to do, Taylor."

"I've got personal reasons for wanting to stay a bit longer. Cut me some slack."

"Personal reasons? Oh, for cryin' out loud. Don't tell me you're screwing one of the boys on the job. Taylor, I warned you about that. You keep away from those boys."

"No. He's not one of the boys here. He's someone I met. Look, I know how you feel about me being gay—" Taylor had to stop his father's tirade in its tracks before it started, "Dad! Listen to me!" After getting his father's attention, Taylor continued, "I never ask nothin' from you other than a damn paycheck. We don't have no relationship as father and son. Shut up and hear me out!" Taylor yelled, then calmed his voice. "I'm asking you to cut me some slack this time. I can't leave. Not yet."

After a long strained silence, his father said, "I'll send Noah to Cleveland to start. But I'm giving him a week. If he can't get them on target, you go. You got that? I don't give a rat's ass about your demented love-life. The job comes first. One week."

Knowing it was better than he expected, Taylor muttered, "Whatever." The line disconnected. Shutting down the phone in his hand, Taylor felt like bursting he was so frustrated by the conversation. He stepped inside the trailer and handed the secretary back her phone. "Thank you."

"You okay, Taylor?"

"Yeah, I'm fine." He adjusted his yellow hardhat and headed back outside into the fresh air.

~

His turn to be the excited one, Owen waited for Taylor on the same corner and checked his watch anxiously. When he spotted Taylor making his way toward him, Owen instantly knew something was wrong. That confident strut was gone. Taylor's head was down and his hands were shoved into his front jeans pockets. The man appeared deep in thought. A twinge of worry passed through Owen's mid-section. When they met up on the same corner, Owen kissed Taylor's cheek this time, since Taylor appeared too preoccupied to remember. "What's happened?"

Taylor just gave him a pained look.

Holding open the door to the parking garage, Owen waited until they were seated inside the car before he asked again. "Taylor, did something happen on the site?"

"My dad called. He's trying to get me to go to Cleveland to start another job."

Owen didn't realize the effect that would have on him. Instantly, he felt devastated. "When do you go?"

"I don't know. He gave me one more week." Taylor stared out of the window of the car, his eyes distant and moody.

Starting the engine, Owen drove back to his home in silence. The party was over before it began. No. It couldn't be like this. They needed more time. They were just beginning to connect and become a real couple. No.

Pulling into his driveway, elevating the garage door, Owen parked the car, shutting it off, sitting still for a moment before he climbed out. Taylor didn't. He exited the car quickly and headed inside the house.

When Taylor had left, Owen finally opened his car door. Tiredly and without enthusiasm, he popped the trunk to remove all his parcels, dragging his feet, intending on dumping them on the floor of his bedroom. As Owen walked through his door, he found Taylor on his cell phone, standing in the kitchen.

"Dad, it's me."

Owen lowered his head and left Taylor alone for his conversation, going to the bedroom to change out of his suit.

As he found a hanger for his jacket and slacks, Owen knew he wasn't the only one to have family issues. Obviously Taylor was dealing with his own at the moment. Seeing Taylor facing his problem head on, Owen felt inspired. Once he was in his denims and a soft cotton shirt, Owen sat on his bed and picked up his telephone. "Jenna? It's me. Is Leah available?"

"Why? What are you going to do?"

"She's been sending me text messages about meeting Taylor. I can't keep letting her think he's a she. I feel like crap about it."

"So now you're going to tell her about it over the phone after all?"

"What choice do I have? Jenna, she'll be really pissed off at me if I let her believe this person is a woman all week long. I think the lie will be worse than the truth."

"You better be tactful about it, Owen. She's only ten."

"Jenna, stay on the line with us. Okay? Help me."

"Okay. Hang on."

Owen rubbed his face in agony having no idea how Leah was going to react.

~

"Pop, please, I don't ask you for nothing. I don't. I couldn't stand the way we left it off earlier. Please, hear me out. Don't get all angry and hang up like that."

"Taylor..."

Taylor hated that tone. He'd heard it through his

122

childhood, and it always annoyed him. "Pop, I can't understand you. You put up with Jason, and he's nothin' but a high school drop-out who can't do anything more than part time work. Ya put up with Leslie who drinks like a damn fish and won't go to rehab. Me? I work like a dog for you. I go anywhere ya send me. I'm the only one of the four of us boys who ya trust enough to work for you as a project manager. Luke and Caleb are just laborers, Pop. Ya got them digging trenches. So obviously I'm the one you count on."

"You're the oldest Taylor."

"Yeah, the oldest and the wisest. I never set out to disappoint ya, Pop, you know that."

After a long silence, Mr. Madison asked, "What is so different about this one? Why do you need to stay there?"

Looking back at the closed bedroom door first, Taylor then whispered, "I love this man, Pop. I didn't love anyone before."

"Love?"

"Yeah. I mean it. He's the right one. He's unbelievable, Pop."

"What's he do?"

"He's got his own business. He's an accountant. Very successful. Got a big house in LA, a Lexus. You'd like the fella."

"He like one of them fairies?"

"No. Not at all. He's all man." Taylor looked back at the door, praying Owen wasn't listening to this conversation.

"What do you want me to do, Taylor?"

"Let me hang out 'til completion on this one. Look, trust Noah. He's a good man. He'll do you right in Cleveland."

"Let me think about it."

"It's all I ask, Pop. It's all I ask." Taylor ran his hand back through his hair.

~

"Hello, sweetheart."

"Hi, Daddy!"

"Did you have a good day at school today?" Owen had no idea how he was going to do this.

"Yes. I learned all my multiplication tables. Want to test me?"

"What's nine times nine?"

"Eighty-one!"

"Good girl. Look, Leah, your mom and I have something we need to discuss with you." Owen could hear Jenna's breathing over the line.

"Oh? What?"

"You know I told you about Taylor?" Owen asked gently.

"Yes. I can't wait to meet her."

"Well," Owen took a deep breath. "Taylor isn't a woman, Leah. He's a man."

Silence followed. Owen wondered if Jenna was going to chime in at any moment and tell Leah that all this was perfectly normal. No one said a word.

"Leah," Owen asked, "did you hear what I said?"

"Yes. You said Taylor was a man."

"Yes."

"So, how can he be your girlfriend?"

Jenna, where are you? Owen bit his lip, trying to give his ex a chance to help, but it wasn't happening. "He's your dad's best friend, Leah."

"Oh. Okay."

"Jenna," Owen asked her, "is that okay with you?"

"Yes, Owen," she replied dryly, as if this whole conversation was irritating.

"Good. Well, then, Leah, some day soon you will meet my friend, Taylor. Okay?"

"Okay. Can I go play with Faith now, Mom?"

"Yes," Jenna replied.

Owen heard Leah hang up her extension. "What do you think, Jenna?"

"Look, Owen, just leave it like that for now. I don't think Leah needs the gory details at her age."

"Okay. I just want to do what's best. I don't want her to think I'm lying to her or betraying her."

"I don't think she'll get that. Not at her age."

"Okay. Thanks, Jenna."

"Owen?"

"Yes?"

"Is this what you really want? A relationship with a man?"

Smiling, looking back at the closed bedroom door, Owen replied, "Yes. I feel like I've finally found myself, Jenna. No offense."

"None taken. Look, if you're happy…"

"I am."

"Okay, let me go. I have to get dinner started. See you Friday night."

"See ya." Owen hung up and sat still, thinking about the conversation.

~

Taylor listened at the door. Owen had stopped talking. He rapped on it lightly.

"Come in," Owen called.

Opening the door, Taylor found Owen sitting on the bed near the phone. "You okay?"

"Yes. How about you?"

"Yeah." Taylor sat next to him, leaning on Owen's shoulder.

"Were you talking to your dad?"

"Yes. I just wanted him to stop pushing me to get off the job here. He's got another project manager to handle the next one, and it pisses me off he thinks I have to go to each one of his new sites. Noah's a great man. He can do the damn job."

"But I suppose one day you will be done in LA and need to move on."

Nodding, Taylor looked into Owen's soft brown eyes. "Yes. I will have to pack up and leave the job site once it's complete, Owen. That's inevitable."

Owen reached for Taylor's hand. "What will we do then?"

Shrugging, Taylor answered, "See each other over the weekends? When you visit Leah?"

Owen's face darkened. "I can't do that. I have to spend the time with her, Taylor. It's not fair to her if I see you the whole time I'm in Denver."

Falling back on the mattress, Taylor stared at the ceiling and sighed. "Then I guess it's done."

"No," Owen whined, lying next to Taylor on the bed. "It can't be done."

Taylor rubbed his face tiredly. "What else do you suggest?"

"Can you move to LA?"

Peeking through his hands at him, Taylor said, "Move here?"

Owen shrugged, looking anxious.

"Why don't you move to Denver? Be closer to your daughter?" When Owen didn't answer right away, Taylor added, "Look, we have a bit more time. Let's let it ride for now."

Owen cuddled against Taylor's chest. "And I had such a cool surprise for you tonight. I just don't know if we're in the right mood for it now."

"Surprise? What surprise?" Taylor's solemn mood instantly vanished.

"You know…" Owen nudged him.

"No." Taylor rolled over to be able to see Owen's face. "What? What did you have in mind?"

"Stuff!"

"Well, get to it!" Taylor shoved him. "I'm always up for something fun."

"Yeah?"

"Yeah! Go! Do it. What have you got in mind?"

As if he had renewed enthusiasm, Owen stood off the bed and said, "Wait there. Don't move."

"I'm waiting here." When Owen vanished into the walk-in closet, Taylor did his best to ignore the thoughts of them separating. They'd manage to work it out somehow.

~

Owen felt very odd. Leather? Other than leather shoes and a jacket, what did he own that was cowhide? Sliding his hands down the slick black surface of his thighs, Owen shook his head in awe. Never in his wildest dreams as a pimple-faced teenager did he imagine being the object of someone's sexual fantasy. It was inconceivable. Wishing he had a mirror and could make sure he didn't look ridiculous, Owen ran his hand back through his hair, then opened another bag to dig out the rest of his "equipment".

~

Taylor was almost nodding off as he lay back on the large, soft bed. The sensation of floating was washing over him when he heard the closet door open. Trying to wake up, Taylor caught sight of Owen and sat up instantly. "Holy crap."

Owen grinned wickedly. "You like?"

"What do you plan on doing with all that?"

"Well…" Owen held up some leather straps. "Tie you up with these."

"And that?" Taylor pointed to something that looked like a ping-pong paddle.

"Whack your butt?"

Taylor broke up laughing. "Get over here." He curled his finger in invitation.

Owen set the things on the bed, standing next to them. "No good?"

When Taylor read the disappointment in Owen's face, he got up and began taking off his clothing, watching Owen watching him.

"You sure?" Owen asked. "You know we both just had some weird phone conversations."

"Shut up and get the lube." Taylor winked, continuing to

drop his clothing to the carpet. As Owen hurried to set out the items he thought they would need, Taylor wondered how far he wanted to go with this little fantasy. Staring at Owen's outfit, the skin-tight, black leather pants, the black choker collar, and black boots, Taylor was enjoying looking at him and could feel his body respond.

Pushing his hair back from his forehead, as if he were already heated up, Owen paused in his preparation, asking, "That everything?"

"What have you got?" Taylor walked over to the nightstand to see what was accumulated there. "Looks good."

"Baby oil?" Owen offered.

"Up to you."

"No. This is your fantasy. Remember? I did the one with the chaps."

"Is it?" Taylor found that amusing. Was it his fantasy? He would soon find out. Taking the rest of his clothing off, Taylor asked, "What do you want me to do?"

"Lie on the bed."

"Face up or down?"

Owen instantly appeared perplexed.

As Taylor waited for an answer, he said, "I sure as shit hope that paddle was for my ass and nothing else."

"It was, but if you're face down I can't play with your dick."

"Amateur!" Taylor teased. "What kind of fantasy is this when the damn master can't decide what to do with his victim?"

Appearing insulted, Owen grabbed the paddle and went after Taylor. Laughing as he dodged the swings to his derriere, Taylor raced around the room with Owen in pursuit. Once Taylor was standing on top of the mattress, fending off the attempted slaps from him, Owen shouted, "Just lie on your back. I'll spank you some other time."

"You will not. Not if I can help it." Taylor slowly lowered down on the bed.

Tossing the paddle to the floor, Owen reached for the leather straps and waited.

Slightly nervous about his first foray into being a helpless victim, Taylor stretched out his limbs to the four corners of the bed. One by one, Owen tied him to it. Once Taylor was secure, Owen stood back to stare at him, again pushing his soft hair back from his forehead.

"Now what?" Taylor asked.

"Uh…" Owen crossed his arms over his chest, as if thinking.

Again Taylor began laughing. "Christ, Owen, rent a fucking porno movie. Get some tips!"

"Hey! Be nice. You're at my mercy now."

"Well?" Taylor tried to gesture for Owen to get on with it. "I'm naked and tied to the bed, Owen. I'm not even hard at the moment. Ya gotta start somewhere."

Biting his lip, Owen left the room.

Taylor was confused. He shouted after him, "I didn't mean to insult you. Where the hell are you going?" Trying to listen, Taylor added, "You're not going to just leave me here like this!"

After a short pause, Owen returned, closing the bedroom door behind him.

"Well? Come up with any ideas?"

Holding out a bottle of chocolate syrup, Owen grinned wickedly.

"Am I dessert?" Taylor chuckled as Owen sat next to him on the bed. "We ain't even had dinner yet."

"Life's short, eat dessert first." Owen opened the top and held it up over Taylor's cock.

Lifting his head off the pillows, Taylor watched as a cold, brown stream of liquid dripped on his body. Keeping silent, wondering what he would do once Owen began licking that sweet stuff off, Taylor waited. Suddenly the excitement did stir in him, and his body began to react.

~

Owen set the bottle down. When he turned back, he found Taylor completely erect. "Aha!" Owen accused as he pointed it out.

"Shut up."

"Amateur, am I?" Owen chided. "I don't think so." Owen leaned down over Taylor's chocolate-covered cock and licked it. "Yum."

"I'll say."

Before he began the act of sexual teasing, Owen leaned up on his elbows and said, "By the way. You know, because you're all bound up, if by any chance I do something you don't like, just tell me."

"I doubt that's going to happen."

"I know. But if I were the one tied up, I'd want you to know when I wasn't happy, or if it got too much."

"Okay, Owen."

"So, how about if you want me to stop and cut you loose, you just say…uh…"

"Cowboy."

"Yeah. Cowboy."

"Okay. Now will ya get to it?"

"My pleasure." Owen moved around the bed so he could crawl from the bottom to settle down between Taylor's legs. Holding the base of Taylor's cock, Owen began licking the chocolate sauce off very slowly and lightly with the tip of his tongue. Hearing a low groan coming out of Taylor, Owen smiled happily. Taking his time, Owen cleaned all the sweet syrup off him with his mouth, enjoying the taste of Taylor's skin and the scent of his body. Once he had a good, slow bout of sucking, Owen sat up and stared at Taylor. As he did, Taylor opened his eyes to look back at him.

Without a word, Owen picked up the chocolate bottle and dripped some on Taylor's nipples. Taylor's chest began to rise and fall more rapidly as he appeared to struggle not to pant.

Once Taylor's chest was running with brown syrup,

Owen set the bottle down and began lapping the sweetness off Taylor's hard nipples, nipping them after he had sucked on them until they were rock hard.

Peeking up at Taylor, Owen found him opening and closing his fists as if he were trying to control his excitement. "Still doing okay? Are the straps too tight on your hands?"

"Doing okay. No."

By the concise answer, Owen knew Taylor most likely wanted to stay inside the fantasy and not be reminded they weren't really S and M types. Or were they? *No, no putting out cigarettes on skin. No. Ew.*

Owen got busy again. After both nipples were clean of chocolate, he sat up once more. "Wish I could spank your ass."

Taylor chuckled, keeping his eyes closed.

Owen stood off the bed and looked down at Taylor's entirety. He was so big, so muscular, and so beautiful, Owen wanted to be the submissive one, to kneel on the floor and beg Taylor to always be his. But that wasn't part of the fantasy. Not this one, anyhow.

Moving back to the foot of the bed, Owen leaned down and kissed the bottoms of Taylor's feet, gently, softly. Making his way to Taylor's shins, Owen ran those tender kisses up both legs until he was at Taylor's hips again. Taylor was already straddled wide from the straps tying him to the bed. Nuzzling his face into Taylor's balls, Owen rubbed his rough jaw on them, waiting to see if the word "cowboy" would be spoken. It wasn't.

Continuing to massage them with his scratchy dark shadow, as Owen roughed them up a little, Taylor's legs tensed and his back arched off the bed. Owen stopped. Was it too hard? Nothing was said. He continued what he was doing. A soft moan met his ears. Obviously, he was on the right track. The bed creaked as Taylor strained against the bindings. Pausing, Owen reached for the tube of lubrication on the nightstand. Using a dab, he wet his finger and lowered back down to be at crotch level with Taylor. Going back to using his rough jaw and cheeks on Taylor's genitals, Owen slipped his index finger inside Taylor and smoothed it in and out. The bed creaked again, straining under the power of the captive on top of it. More sounds of pleasure emerged from Taylor's lips. Owen held onto Taylor's cock with his left hand, again using his face to tease Taylor's soft skin. His right index finger kept up a rhythm, in and out of Taylor's butt, massaging as it did, all the right spots inside him.

"Ahh," Taylor whimpered, his hips elevating once more.

Owen felt his own body surge. His cock was bent to the side in his tight leathers throbbing with his beating heart. Continuing to finger-fuck Taylor, Owen slipped Taylor's cock inside his mouth. Instantly he tasted the pre-come drop. Thinking Taylor had waited long enough, Owen sucked harder, pushing his finger deeper as he did. Taylor came, grunting and tensing all his muscles. The wooden frame withstood the pulling from Taylor's arms as he flexed his biceps.

Owen knelt up, staring down at that sight. Opening his leather pants, Owen took out his cock and began masturbating, staring at this unbelievable man.

As Taylor recuperated, Owen shot come all over Taylor's crotch. Sated beyond his wildest expectations, Owen panted to catch his breath, opening his eyes. Taylor was staring at him. And that look was worth its weight in gold.

Owen stripped off his leather pants, boots, tossed the dog-collar on the floor, then crawled over Taylor's body to lie on top of him. Before he untied the bindings, Owen whispered, "I...I..."

Through his own breathy gasps, Taylor asked, "You, you?"

"I...I..."

Taylor began laughing, but it was mixed with exhaustion. "You what, baby?"

"Nothing." Owen couldn't tell him. He felt like an idiot.

Sitting up, he untied Taylor's arms and legs, dropping the straps to the floor. Once Taylor was free, he wrapped around Owen's naked body and cuddled him close. "I know, Owen. I know."

Closing his eyes in relief, Owen felt so much love for Taylor, it hurt.

Chapter Eleven

On Friday morning both of their moods soured. Owen had done his best to pretend the arrangement was permanent, and that every night for the rest of his life he could sleep with the man of his dreams and any worry he may have had of being unloved or alone would vanish.

Then Friday showed up.

Attending a meeting for an audit he had scheduled, Owen felt distracted and not at his best. As he sat with the representative of the IRS and his nervous client, Barry, Owen went through the paperwork to explain deductions, exemptions, and allowances, all the while he was dreading the inevitable day when Taylor left on a Friday night and never came back to LA.

~

Taylor didn't mind Fridays. On the site most of the guys were more relaxed with the impending weekend, and some left early to get a head start on the traffic. The construction disasters had subsided substantially since the beginning of the project, and the initial disagreements between contractors had smoothed out. Everyone seemed to know what they needed to do, and he was left alone to read over the specs and double check measurements and building codes. He knew damn well it was time for him to leave and for Noah to take over. The guilt started gnawing at him. He considered himself a good man, a good employee, and a good son. By dragging out the weeks he needed to spend in LA, he was none of the above. Sitting down in the portable, in the relative quiet of its interior, Taylor took off his hardhat and rubbed his weary face. He just didn't know what the hell to do.

~

By four-thirty Owen looked up from his desk and found Taylor's strained expression as he stood at the doorway. "Out early?"

Taylor nodded. "I usually am on Friday. Gives me a chance to pack and get the rental car back to the airport."

"We already packed, and you don't have a rental car." Owen took his headset off and pushed back his chair from his desk.

"Old habits die hard."

Owen stood and walked closer to him, caressing Taylor's hair along the side of his head. "We have a little time before we have to head to the airport. Want to catch dinner out?"

"No. You mind if we don't? I'm really tired."

Staring at his worn expression, Owen grew upset. "Let me get going then. We can relax at my place first."

"Good. Thank you."

As he shut down his computer and straightened his desk, Owen became concerned. He knew Taylor well enough to know this wasn't just about them not seeing each other over the weekend. It was more. Trying not to bombard Taylor with all his insecurities and fears about them never seeing each other again, Owen kept quiet and finished what he was doing.

Nodding to Taylor he was done, Owen shut off the office light and followed Taylor into the hall. Owen never lost interest in Taylor's masculine gait and the way his soft jeans hugged the curves of his ass. Fantastic.

Quiet in the elevator, quiet on the way home in the car, it was becoming obvious to Owen things were not good. Once they had walked through the door to Owen's kitchen, he finally asked, "Did you talk to your father again?"

"No." Taylor continued on his way to the bedroom.

Removing his tie, Owen began changing his clothing for the flight later that night. "Taylor, I can tell something is bothering you."

After kicking off his shoes, Taylor stretched out on Owen's bed, placing his hands behind his head.

Owen finished changing, wishing Taylor would just tell him what was on his mind. Once Owen had double-checked that he had packed everything he needed, and they had both printed their e-tickets from the computer, Owen dropped down to lie next to Taylor on the bed. "It's about LA. It's about you having to leave."

Taylor inhaled deeply but didn't reply.

Rolling over so he could see him more clearly, and touch him, Owen smoothed his hand over Taylor's chest, enjoying how solid his body was. "Are you feeling guilty for sticking around? Is that it?"

A frown found its way to Taylor's lips.

Owen knew he hit the mark. "Then go, Taylor. Don't do something you'll regret for me. Go. We'll see each other again."

"When?" Taylor shouted, biting his lip as if he were upset with himself for being so angry.

"I have some vacation time." Owen shrugged.

Taylor twisted away so his back was facing Owen. Owen could just about see fumes coming off of Taylor he was so upset.

Cuddling closer, Owen spooned Taylor from behind, wrapping his arms around to hug him. "Where is the next job?"

"Cleveland."

"Crap. Cleveland?"

"Yeah."

Owen couldn't even imagine a reason he could make up to go there. It didn't matter. What mattered was Taylor. "You want me to come with you? It could be our little vacation."

Feeling Taylor pushing back to roll over again, Owen backed up and allowed him. When he caught Taylor's eyes, he knew he'd said something absurd.

Taylor replied, "Cleveland. You want us to spend our vacation in Cleveland instead of the U.K. Are you some kinda nut?"

"Hey," Owen defended, "I'm just trying to figure out a way we can be together. Don't take it out on me. I'm not the one with work in another state."

Standing off the bed abruptly, Taylor left the room in a huff.

Pausing in his wake, Owen didn't want it to end like this. No. Not like this. "What am I saying? I don't want it to end at all!" He jumped off the bed and ran out of the room.

He found Taylor drinking a shot of brandy from a carafe Owen had set out in the dining room, "for emergency purposes only". *This qualified.*

"Taylor. Please. Tell me what you want me to do."

The empty glass in his hand, Taylor replied, "It don't matter."

"It does matter! For crying out loud, Taylor!"

As he refilled the tiny shot glass, Taylor said, "I can't tell you what to do. I can't. It'd be like someone telling me to do something. I can't live that way. A man does what he wants. Not what someone tells him to do. That's why I don't listen to anything anybody tells me anymore. Not since I was a little boy and my mama told me what to do. Well, guess what, Owen, I ain't a little boy anymore and neither are you. We're big grown-ups now, Owen, and no one tells us nothin'!"

Hating to say it, Owen giggled, "Man, your Texas accent is if full swing at the moment."

"Shut up," Taylor shouted, but a smile edged through.

"Give me one of those." Owen reached for the glass.

"You're drivin'. No way." Taylor held it back. "Have a Guinness at the airport."

Nodding in agreement, Owen dropped his hand to his

side and watched as Taylor took one more swig, then capped the carafe and set the glass down.

"Okay, Taylor, you're right. We are men, and we should make our own decisions."

"Yes." Taylor wiped his mouth with the back of his hand.

"Good. Tell me what you want me to do."

Blinking first, Taylor then doubled over with laughter, holding his side.

Owen was very glad he had made him laugh. "I already know what I have to do, Taylor. I already know."

Slowing his laughing fit, Taylor stood up straight and his face became deadly serious again. "I'm not asking you. I did before, and it was wrong. You're settled here. You got clients to think of, to take care of."

"I do. But life's all about priorities, Taylor. And if I am, as you say, all grown-up, which to be honest I don't feel in the least, but that's another story…"

"Fast forward, Owen." Taylor spun his finger around like a circle.

"What I'm saying is, if I move to Denver, then I'll be near both you and Leah."

Taylor didn't speak, just stared at Owen.

Owen was waiting. Wasn't there supposed to be a celebration? A whooping it up and a high-five slap in victory. Did he get it all wrong again?

"We should get going." Taylor brushed past Owen to the hall where their suitcases were setting.

"Taylor," Owen followed him, "aren't you going to say something?"

"I can't."

"You can't?" Owen took his keys out of his pocket and shut off the interior lights of the kitchen.

"No."

Perplexed as usual, Owen opened the trunk of the car and they placed their bags inside. Once they were backing out of the drive and on their way to the airport, Owen asked, "Why not?"

~

Taylor rubbed his eyes in agony. How could he make that decision for Owen? How could he influence the man to move, come to Denver, only to find he was on the road so much they would hardly see each other? "Fine!" Taylor shouted in frustration. "You do what you think is best, Owen. But I have to warn you, I travel a hell of a lot."

"Like how much?"

"How long do you think I've been gone working on this project?"

Owen put on his thinking face. "Two weeks?"

"Four. Next one's in Cleveland. 'Bout four to five more. Then I have to ask myself where's my daddy going to send me next? You see? So, say you move. Okay? It sounds perfect, and believe me, Owen, I want you there in Denver. More than you can ever know. Okay, you make that change. You sell your gorgeous house in LA, make the move, say bye-bye to your clients, or whatever...okay? You come stay with me, 'cause you will, you will stay with me. I wouldn't have it any other way." Taylor looked over at Owen's profile as he drove, merging onto the highway. "I get an assignment, and off I go. That leaves you alone, waiting for me."

"Don't you trust me?"

"What? What the hell are you talking about? Trust you? With my goddamn life. I'm not talking about trust. I'm talking about getting you all the way out to Denver and leaving you on your own for a month."

As he drove Owen kept peering over at Taylor, a look of disbelief on his face.

Taylor threw up his hands at the lack of a comment from Owen.

~

Owen was suspicious. He didn't like the conversation one bit. Didn't Taylor realize he was already alone in LA? Did Taylor see even a part-time companion and lover hanging around? There had to be another reason for his setting up that kind of defensive roadblock. And with Owen's track-record of abuse in school and a failed marriage, he was starting to think he needed to be taking the hint here. It was a fling. A fucking fling with a man who was ready to move on to his next conquest. Fine. Screw it.

~

Taylor wondered why Owen wouldn't say anything. Why on earth didn't Owen at least say it was okay even part of the time as long as they were together? Where was that reassurance he craved? And why, when Taylor had been so confident and strong with every other relationship, did he feel like he had "needs" with this one? What was it about Owen that made Taylor feel complete when he was around him?

Following road signs to LAX, the two men rode in silence.

~

Owen felt betrayed. Standing in line at the check-in counter, Taylor just slightly ahead of him in line, Owen wondered if this would begin and end on a plane. It had gotten cold between them. Communication had never been Owen's forte. He was an introvert and hated confrontation. Jenna walked all over him. It was her decision to divorce, move his child from the state, and dictate the rules of their visits and time together. Owen didn't argue. He hated arguing. He agreed to all her terms of alimony, child support, visitation, whatever she wanted. He didn't understand why they had divorced, but he figured she must have her reasons. The geek from high school didn't deserve her anyway. He was lucky she married him in the first place. He was a damn virgin when she met him.

Together Taylor and he approached the counter, handing the woman their printout e-tickets. She clicked away feverishly on her computer, assigning them their usual seats. Taylor handed Owen his boarding pass after giving their bags to the woman to place on the conveyor- belt. Unburdened by luggage, Owen followed Taylor's lead to security. As they emptied their pockets into a tub, Owen watched Taylor pass through the metal detector. Taylor was stopped and patted down. Owen was told to wait before coming through. Witnessing that young man sliding his hands all over his lover's body *again*, Owen grew angry. He didn't want anyone else touching his Taylor. And that was just the security guy! If Taylor found a new boyfriend, Owen would kill someone.

The uniformed man waved Owen through. No one bothered with him. He met Taylor at the end of the x-ray area and filled his pockets with his wallet and keys again, taking his coat from another plastic tub, as Taylor did the same.

"Enjoy your little pat down?" Owen asked sarcastically.

"I get nailed every time."

"Maybe he just wants to feel your balls."

"What the hell's with you? You think I enjoy being touched by some moron?"

"I don't know. Do you?"

"Screw you."

Owen's pout was now firmly planted on his face. Taylor paused and said, "Look, if you don't want to hang around with me, just go and do your own thing."

"Did I say that?" Owen felt crushed.

"No, but you don't have to. You haven't spoken a fucking word to me since I mentioned my business trips."

"You...you..."

"Me? Me? Don't start stuttering on me, Owen."

At the condescending tone, Owen spun on his heels and walked away from Taylor. He was so upset he could burst out crying.

~

In agony as Owen walked away, Taylor held back a shout to call him back. Maybe it was better this way. If Owen didn't want to move to Denver, maybe they should just call it quits and not make some kind of long goodbye.

Seeing Owen vanish in the crowd, Taylor walked to the

bar and ordered himself a Guinness.

~

Owen felt his emotions welling up to embarrassing proportions. Stepping inside a men's room, he stood in a stall and tried to bite back his tears with everything he had. Memories washed over him. Crying in the bathroom in school when bullies had teased him about his braces, being singled out for his shyness, his fear of asking a girl to a dance or out on a date.

Wiping at his eyes roughly, Owen felt as if he hadn't matured a day from fourteen. Inside, he was still the same pimply, ugly kid. And even though he had managed to marry a pretty woman and now had a great looking man interested in him, Owen didn't feel his appeal justified that attention. Inhaling, knowing he had to get to the gate sooner or later, Owen left the bathroom stall and washed his hands and face at the sink. When he looked up into the mirror, his eyes were red and watery, and though others in the world may see a handsome man, Owen found a homely misfit in the reflection. Wiping his hands and face on a paper towel, Owen stood tall and decided it didn't matter what people thought. Many people cried at airports when they separated from loved ones. It didn't matter.

~

A Guinness at his mouth, Taylor felt sick inside. Brainstorming on ways to stop the constant traveling he had to do out of state, he tried to think of other types of employment he was capable of. Job hunt? Did he want to do that when Daddy was paying him a six-figure salary? Where was he going to get another job he loved for that kind of money? Originally, he hadn't minded traveling. He had no reason to stay home. He did now. And the dilemma was literally killing him.

When he noticed someone standing near his tiny round table, he raised his head. Owen was staring down at him, his expression so lost and upset it devastated Taylor.

Placing the glass of beer down with a clatter, Taylor stood up and embraced Owen. When he did, he felt Owen's body begin to shake with his tears. "Shh, all right. Sit down. Let's talk."

As Owen looked around the area, dabbing at his eyes discreetly, Taylor made sure he sat down first, handing him the rest of his beer. "Look, Owen, obviously we have to work this out. It's killing us."

"What's to work out?" Owen sipped Taylor's beer. "You said you travel and you don't want me to move to Denver."

"I didn't say that." Taylor cringed at how his words were interpreted. "I just said I was afraid if you made that leap to live with me, you might find yourself on your own."

"I don't care. I'll wait for you."

Smiling warmly, Taylor reached out to wipe the beer-foam mustache from Owen's top lip. "You will? You'd do that for me?"

"Are you as stupid as you sound?" Owen asked in exasperation.

"I guess so." Taylor chuckled softly.

They heard a boarding call for their flight. Owen finished the rest of the beer and gestured for them to get going.

"We have time. You want to grab another one?" Taylor pointed to the bar.

"No, I'll get one on the flight."

As they headed to their gate, Taylor put his arm around Owen's waist. He loved this man and didn't care who figured it out. "You okay?"

Owen nodded, smiling at him bravely. "Better now that you're not dumping me."

"Dumping you? That's the last thing on my mind." Taylor squeezed him tight.

Standing in the dull line as passengers were called by zone and seat number to board, Taylor kept a sharp eye on Owen. It seemed to Taylor, Owen was still upset and more talking was in order. Well, they had two and a half hours on a

143

plane to do it.

Making sure his hand was in contact with Owen as he moved down the narrow aisle of the body of the plane, Taylor pressed up against the back of him whenever Owen paused to allow someone to get into their seat or stow a bag overhead. Not only did he love the contact, he wanted to keep reassuring Owen that this was anything but a goodbye.

Finally at their seat number, Owen entered first to be near the window, sitting down as Taylor waited to do the same. Once they were both comfortable, Owen whispered, "Feng shui."

Grinning, as if the spell of doom had been broken, Taylor nodded. "Feng shui. You notice we sleep on the same side of the bed as well?"

Owen paused, as if he was visualizing it. "You're right. I'm on the left and you're on the right. Amazing. It would feel wrong if we switched."

Finding Owen's hand, Taylor replied, "It would feel wrong if we didn't stay together."

"I agree. Taylor, I'd be lost without you."

Taking a quick look around the area, Taylor pecked Owen on the lips. "Ditto."

"Wow, that was bold." Owen sat up and checked to see if there were any frowning faces.

"Not bold. Not when you love a man."

Owen twisted in the seat to stare at Taylor in amazement. "Do you really love me?"

Savoring that innocence, Taylor answered, "I really do, Mr. Braydon."

"Wow. I mean, wow." Owen rubbed his forehead as if the notion were astounding him.

"So? You going to move to Denver? Is that the plan?"

Biting his lip, Owen nodded. "I guess so. I mean, I have to admit when Jenna took Leah out of state, I did imagine following them. But at the time, it was so nasty the way Jenna did it, I felt defiant about not allowing her to make that

Taylor smiled. It was the sign that Owen wanted to play. "Right, so this Jenna, she just up and leaves you with your daughter in tow. No explanation other than, 'I need space'?"

Spreading the blanket out over both their laps, Owen nodded. "Swear to god. That was it."

"There must be something I don't know about you," Taylor teased.

"Maybe she knew something about me I didn't know about myself."

"How's that?" Taylor tilted his head in question.

"I'm gay. Taylor, I'm very gay. I can't believe how much I'm enjoying sex with you. Not only the physical part of this relationship, but the male companionship. I love the man in you. I obviously couldn't love the man in Jenna."

"So you think Jenna knew you were gay before you did?" Taylor felt Owen's hand move to his lap under the blue flannel.

"Yes. Maybe. There could have been signs. I don't know. Maybe I stared at the television too long when Brad Pitt was on."

Taylor started laughing. "Yeah, that's always the indication a man is gay. Owen, shut up."

"What do you want me to do? Ask her? Say, Hey, Jenna, my new boyfriend wants to know why you dumped me? Did I snore? Pick my nose in public?"

"I know you don't snore. And I haven't seen ya pick your nose in public yet, so that ain't going to help me."

~

Owen began to get insulted. "Wait a minute. Are you serious about trying to find out why Jenna didn't want to be around me, so you can find out if you can tolerate what she couldn't?"

"Why do you say such stupid things? Owen, that's ridiculous."

"Then why are you so curious as to why she divorced me?"

"Ever screw a woman?"

"No. Never have."

"Huh." That surprised Owen. He wondered if in the back of Taylor's mind he would always wonder what that would be like and eventually want to find out.

"I can tell what you're thinking."

Owen asked in surprise, "You can?"

"Yes. The answer is no." Taylor drank more of his beer from the bottle. "I bet it's chicken and ravioli again."

"Back the truck up, Taylor. Don't change the subject on me. You said the answer was no. What did you think my question was going to be?"

"Do I want to know what it's like to have sex with a woman? The answer to that, Owen, is no."

Owen was impressed. It was indeed what he was thinking. "Why not?"

"I just don't have the inclination. Why do you think I'm gay?"

"Yes, but don't most men start out liking woman, or trying to like women, and then find out they're gay?"

"Did you read that in one of your college books?" Taylor raised an eyebrow.

"No. It's just Braydon-logic."

"Well, maybe it's logical for some fellas, but not me. I've preferred men since I was a small boy. I knew early on it was men for me."

"Really?" Owen found that hard to swallow. Most young boys suffered from peer pressure and parental influence. At least he had.

"It wasn't easy, Owen, being the oldest of six. And my brothers always looked up to me. I had to set a damn example. I couldn't be caught dead kissing another boy."

"Wow. That's harsh."

"You have no idea."

"Well, I sort of do, because of what you've said about your dad." Owen's wine went down too quickly and he craved another.

"He's not nearly as bad as when he first found out. Almost skinned me alive."

"How did he find out?"

"You really want to hear all this?"

Owen rubbed Taylor's leg under the blanket. "Yes. But not if you don't want to tell me."

"I don't mind. Hell, you're my partner now. You should be able to ask me anything."

His chest swelling in pride, Owen blushed again. *I love the sound of that!*

"Right. I'll tell ya. We hired a young man to help us break a horse Pop had bought at an auction. At first Pop said he didn't care if anyone could ride him, since he was just for stud. But after a few days, I knew he'd want the stallion broken. I tried, Luke tried, Caleb tried, Jason…no use. None of us could break him. So, Pop finds some fella from a neighboring ranch and asks him. I swear, Owen, when I set eyes on him, I creamed my jeans."

Owen had already left the real world and was floating around in some Hollywood Western movie. Maybe it was *A River Runs Through It*, or *Brokeback Mountain*. Wherever it was, gorgeous cowboys abound. *Oh, there'd be a huge mansion on acres of land. Horses everywhere. Cowpokes sitting on fences in faded torn denim, boots and spurs, hats and chaps. Oh, definitely chaps! And there'd be tons of men. Dusty, callused men with unshaven jaws. They'd all walk like they were just fucking something for hours…*

"Owen?"

"Huh?"

"You listening?"

"Yes!"

"Right. Well, this fella comes in to break this crazy black horse we got. I swear the horse's eyes would go bright red when someone tried to ride him. No matter what we did to tie him up, he'd go ballistic. So, Tristan—"

"Tristan?" Owen interrupted. "Did you say this guy's name was 'Tristan'?"

"Yeah, anyway, we get the horse ready for him. I swear I've never seen a man ride like he did. He had that horse eating out of the palm of his hand in a matter of minutes. Once he breaks the damn stallion, he climbs off and gives the horse's nose a good rub in appreciation. I'd never seen a man do what he did. So, there's me, salivating over him like he's the damnedest thing I'd ever seen..."

Owen was so hot he was about to die. *Brad Pitt? No, Jake Gyllenhaal? No, oh, god who would play that part? Owen Wilson?*

"You still with me?" Taylor asked.

"Huh? Yes. Sorry, go on."

"Well, I was a mere pup then, Owen. I was sixteen. I'd never touched anyone before, not girl nor boy. When Tristan was leaving, I ran after him. Pop had already paid him. He had his money and was about to get into his truck. I actually had the balls to stop that man from getting into his rig. I told him, in no uncertain terms, he floated my boat. I didn't care who knew, who he told, or if he punched my lights out."

"Wow..." Owen's eyes were wide and his hand was once again between Taylor's legs.

"Instead of beatin' the shit out of me, he hops out of his truck, looks around, and signals me to come into one of the empty horse stalls. There he unzipped his jeans and let me suck him. I was sold ever since. Only problem was my kid brother, Caleb, was spying on us. Went right to Pop with it. Damn near killed me. But it was worth it. Worth the first blowjob. I never forgot it."

"You and Jake Gyllenhaal?"

"What? Jake Gyllenhaal? What the hell are you talking about?"

"Move!" Owen shoved him. "Come on, get going."

"What?"

"Go to the damn bathroom and do it now!"

As if Taylor had just figured it out, he erupted with laughter. "I should have guessed. Another one of your cowboy fantasies?"

"Go!"

"I'm going." Taylor unbuckled his belt and laughed the entire walk to the tail of the plane.

Owen waited, *one, two, three, that's enough.* He followed Taylor's path down the aisle, not daring to peek at the occupants as they watched the movie, headphones on, read newspapers, or worked on laptops.

Rapping his knuckles on a door, he waited, pushing at it. "Taylor," he whispered through it. Then realized a second bathroom was also occupied. "Shit." He moved to that one and knocked. It opened instantly and that large masculine hand grabbed his shirt and dragged him in quickly.

"I knocked on the wrong door."

"So what? Now, which part of my story made you so excited?"

"All of it! Holy shit. Was that all real or just a great fantasy for my benefit?"

Taylor's eyes lit up. "I'm sworn to secrecy."

"You devil!" Owen wrapped around him and kissed him, closing his eyes at the pleasure of contacting Taylor that way. As their tongues battled for supremacy, Owen began undoing his pants, dying for a blowjob.

"Christ, we're getting too good at this." Taylor sat on the closed toilet seat and yanked Owen's jeans wider.

"Practice makes perfect." Owen shivered as Taylor sucked on him, Taylor's mouth so hot and wet it was all he needed to shiver down to his shoes. Steadying himself with one hand on the door and one on Taylor's shoulder, all Owen had to do was envision Taylor sucking some cowboy's cock in a horse's stall, and he was there. "Ah!"

Taylor lurched forward to suck harder, as if he was surprised it came on so quickly. He finished the job and then sat back, looking up at Owen. "Wow, you sure were ready."

"No kidding. I almost came in my seat back there. What a story."

"My turn." Taylor switched places, unzipping his jeans.

Sitting on the toilet after getting himself back together, Owen reached out and drew Taylor's cock into his mouth, moaning in delight. It didn't take long for Taylor, either. After a few deep thrusts into Owen's mouth, he climaxed and clenched his teeth to stifle his grunting. It was as if they were both already primed. Sitting up, wiping his mouth with his fingers, Owen smiled at Taylor as he fastened his clothing and tucked in his shirt. "I adore you."

"I adore you, too, Owen, but man, what is your thing for cowboys? Jake Gyllenhaal of *Brokeback Mountain*? Come on. Give me a break."

"Sorry. Soft spot. Ready?"

"Yes." Taylor peeked out, returning to their chairs as if nothing had happened.

Owen followed behind him, actually not caring if the attendants noticed. What would they do? He wasn't a terrorist, and there wasn't a law about sharing a bathroom on a plane. Not that he was familiar with. And if there was? He'd take the risk. Anything to get Taylor's cock in his mouth, and vice versa.

Comfortable once more in their seats, the meal cart making its way towards them, Owen said, "I think I'll be daring and get the ravioli this time. You seemed to like it."

"I did. And it's an excellent second course to come."

"Dirty, dirty..." Owen chided.

"You love it, you rascal."

Owen did. He felt infinitely better about moving to Denver with Taylor's reassurances. There was no choice. He was moving.

chapter Twelve

This time, after they grabbed their bags, Owen and Taylor walked together to the arrival area. Yes, it was premature for Leah to meet Taylor, but she was a resilient kid and she could deal with it. Owen wanted to hold Taylor's hand, but restrained himself to avoid possible grief from Jenna.

"Daddy!"

Owen nudged Taylor and nodded to where his daughter was.

"Cute as a button, Owen." Taylor smiled.

Dropping his bag so he could hug her, Owen spun Leah around and then set her back on her feet. "How are you, sugarplum?"

"Great, Daddy."

Seeing Jenna staring directly at Taylor, Owen announced, "Jenna? This is my good friend, Taylor Madison."

They shook hands briefly.

Leah shouted, "Taylor!"

"Hello, Leah. I've heard so much about you." Taylor patted her head.

"Me, too! Are you coming to stay with us?"

"No, Leah, I got my own home to go to, but we'll be sure to meet up again."

Owen loved the connection, loved it. Moving a step away from his daughter and ex-wife, Owen said to Taylor, "I'll call you. I can't see why, if you have the time, we can't meet for lunch or dinner, you, me, and Leah."

"That would be terrific, Owen." Taylor looked over Owen's shoulder.

"They watching?"

"Yes. Should we skip the kiss?"

"Screw them." Owen pecked him on the lips.

"Call me."

"I will, later." Owen smiled as he watched Taylor wave good-bye and leave.

Wonderful warmth tingling all over his body, Owen turned around, found Leah's cheerful face, and a scowl on Jenna's. "What?"

"A public kiss? You have to be kidding me, Owen," Jenna scolded, gesturing for them to start walking to the short-term parking area.

"Oh, join the twenty-first century, Jenna. Who cares?"

"How about Leah?"

Carrying his case to the escalator, Owen asked his daughter, "Did you mind if Daddy kissed Taylor goodbye?"

"No. He's really cute, Daddy."

"Yes, Leah, he is." Owen stuck his tongue out playfully at Jenna. Even her stern expression had to crack under those circumstances.

Silent until they were seated in the car, Owen noticed Leah in the back seat, instantly involved with her fake computer pet as he buckled his seatbelt. "I have something to discuss with you, Jenna, when we get home."

"Oh? Sounds serious."

"Yes and no."

"About the stud?"

"Yes." Owen chuckled. *Taylor was a stud, oh yes, make no mistake.*

"I can't believe he's gay."

"Me, neither. Damn, good luck on my part, don't you think, Jenna?"

"Don't rub it in," she laughed.

"Why are you taking this so well?" Owen had imagined the complete opposite reaction when she found out.

"Because. Owen, it makes sense."

"It does?" He watched as she merged onto the highway.

"Yes. There were some things, some signs during our marriage."

Peeking behind him quickly, Owen asked, "Can we discuss this later?"

"Yes. Sorry."

Wondering what the hell he could have done to make Jenna think he was gay, Owen had to be content to wait, not wanting his daughter to hear any of that conversation.

~

Back on his way home, Taylor wished Owen were sitting next to him in the truck. He was already missing him. Pulling into his driveway, seeing the darkness of the interior, Taylor had a pang of loneliness and wondered how long it would take for Owen to sell his house in LA and move. Even one day was too long as far as Taylor was concerned. Parking, shutting off the ignition, Taylor climbed out of the truck with his bag and walked with his keys to the front door. Yelling as he always did, "Honey, I'm home!" hearing nothing but his echo in reply, he smiled, knowing those days were going to be gone very soon. He craved a shower, food, and bed.

Flipping on lights as he went, Taylor wondered how Owen would do on sharing his news. It could only be good. He would be closer to his daughter. That had to be something even his ex would think was a positive change.

~

Once Leah was in her bedroom, leaving them alone, Jenna stuck a prepared casserole into the oven. Owen placed his bag down in the den, threw his coat on the couch and met Jenna in the kitchen. He sat down on one of the kitchen chairs and watched as she managed to get them dinner going even though it was late and he knew she was tired. "Jenna?"

"Yes?" She started setting the table.

Owen immediately stood up to help. "Look, I've been thinking about it, and I don't like living so far away from Leah."

She paused, holding a handful of silverware. When he met her eye, she snarled, "Cut the crap, Owen. You're moving here for your lover. Not for your daughter."

"Yeah, well, maybe. But it is good for Leah. You can't deny that."

"I'm not so sure." She set the silverware on the table. "If you and your Taylor-guy are together, you won't see Leah as much as you do now."

"Jenna." Owen wanted to scream her name in rage, but used a calm voice instead. "I can see Leah more if I live here in Denver. And not just for weekends." He folded napkins in half and placed them under the forks.

"What about her weekends?"

"What about them?"

"You'll be with Taylor, won't you? I assume you two work full time. Won't Leah's weekends put a damper on the fun?"

"Please don't be this way, Jenna. I actually thought you were being pretty cool about it until now."

Her expression softened, but she didn't meet his eyes. "It is a good thing for Leah."

"Thank you. Look, you know I'll do my best to be with her as much as I can."

"I know."

Leaning around the doorway, Owen made sure Leah wasn't listening. "What did I do to show you signs I was gay while we were married, Jenna?"

She laughed.

Owen was intrigued. He removed glasses from out of a cupboard and set them on the table.

"You drooled over the men on the television."

"I knew it! Brad Pitt!" Owen laughed with her.

"You used to flip channels, and the minute a male torso showed up, you'd pause, then when a female tit would flash up on the screen, you'd keep flipping. I could never figure it out, Owen. Most men are the exact opposite."

"I had no idea I was doing that." Owen finished setting the table and sat back down on the chair.

"It was more than that. You really didn't enjoy, you know…" She pointed to herself.

"No. I admit that. I didn't."

"Well, most men do, Owen." She took the oven mitts out of a drawer and set them on the counter.

"Is that why you left me?"

"No. It wasn't. I was convinced that was just you. You know, your idiosyncrasies."

"You said you needed more space. Was that it?"

"Yes. You smothered me."

"But…" Owen gestured his frustration with his hands. "You made me feel so insecure. I guess I kept needing you to tell me things were okay."

"I couldn't tell you that, Owen, because things weren't okay."

"Did you cheat?" Owen braced himself, as if he knew the answer. And to his surprise, Jenna was honest.

"Yes. I did. I'm so sorry, Owen."

He thought it would crush him, but it didn't. Either time or Taylor's rich loving had softened the blow.

"I slept with the landscaper."

"Chris? No way!" Owen remembered the young man.

"Sorry. He offered. And he liked, you know." She pointed to herself again.

"Huh." Owen suddenly felt very naïve. "How could I have missed that?"

"We only did it twice, Owen. And you worked full time. It wasn't that hard to hide it."

"Wow." Owen rubbed his face tiredly. "It is harsh, Jenna. I tried really hard. I worked like a dog to get you everything you needed. You and Leah."

"I never faulted you as a provider, Owen." She peeked at the casserole and then shut the oven again. "So, how did you and the Texan meet?"

Smiling, Owen asked, "You hear his accent?"

"*Yes...*" She shook her head as if the comment was silly.

"We met on the plane. He seduced me. Believe it?"

"You have to be kidding. Seduced you? How did he suspect you were gay? Were you drooling over him the way you do over the men on TV?"

"Probably." Owen chuckled. "We're full-fledged members of the Mile High Club."

Covering her ears she shouted, "Too much information!"

"Sorry. I suppose it is tacky." He toyed with a fork that sat on the table.

"No. It's exotic. I can't believe my boring Owen had sex with a man on the plane."

"Does it make you want me again?" He grinned.

"Uh, no. Sorry."

"Are you seeing anyone, Jenna?" Owen asked, standing to get himself a drink.

"Yes. I've been seeing a very nice man for about a year now."

"Why haven't you said anything?" Owen offered Jenna a glass of juice. She nodded and he poured two.

"I suppose I thought it would hurt you."

"You cared if you hurt me after divorcing me?" He replaced the juice container into the fridge and sat back down again.

"Yes. Just because I didn't want to stay married to you any longer doesn't mean I want to see you hurt, Owen."

"Huh..." He drank his juice and thought about it. "What's he do?"

"He works over at the bowling alley. Nothing special."

About to smirk, he stopped himself. "How old is he?"

"None of your business."

"Jenna," he teased, "How old?"

"I said none of your business!" she replied, but was smiling.

"You cradle robber."

"Maybe."

Owen grinned as he thought about it. "Oh well, I suppose we both moved on."

"Yes. And speaking about moving. I assume you'll be living with Taylor?"

"Yes. I've never been to his place, so I have no idea how big it is."

"I bet you do know how big it is."

Meeting her wicked expression, Owen cracked up. "Jenna!"

"Sorry. I couldn't resist."

Right after she opened the oven to check on dinner, Owen stood and hugged her. "Thank you. You're being really cool about this."

"It's okay, Owen. I think it is really cool. And Taylor seems like a sweetheart."

Releasing her, Owen asked, like he was a kid asking his mom, "Can I invite him over for dinner with us this weekend?"

"Sure. I'd love to get to know him better."

"Let me ask Leah." Owen leapt in the air in excitement.

"Go!" Jenna waved him out.

Racing up the stairs to his daughter's room, Owen knocked and asked softly, "Can I come in, sweetie?"

"Sure, Dad."

He pushed back the door to see her pink ruffled room. Heart shaped-velvet pillows were stacked on her canopy bed, little plastic horses and stuffed toys lined her dressers. "Hey, pumpkin."

"What's up, Daddy? Is dinner done? I'm starved."

He sat on the floor where had a pad with magic markers out, drawing colorful pictures. "Soon. I know we eat late on Fridays. Do you mind?"

"I like to wait for you."

"You are so good to me." He petted her hair back. "I have a favor to ask you."

"Okay."

"Would it be okay if Taylor comes to dinner with us over our weekend? Mom said it was okay with her."

"Sure!"

Seeing her drawing of animals on the pad, Owen said, "Did you know Taylor's dad owns horses?"

"He does? Can I see them?"

"His dad lives in Texas." Owen reached for a marker and drew out a map of the States. "See. We are here." He drew a circle on the map, then a line to where Texas should be. "And Taylor's daddy lives *all* the way down here."

"Oh."

"But...Taylor can tell you all about them. He's really good with telling stories."

"Okay. Is it time to eat yet?"

"Come on, let's check." Owen stood up, reaching out his hand.

~

A beer in his fist, Taylor reclined in his den, watching the news. Yawning, checking his watch, when the phone rang, he smiled in expectation. Picking it up, he said, "Hello?"

"Heya, good lookin'."

"Hello, Mr. Braydon. You sound chipper. Things going well?"

"Fantastic. I swear, it's strange. Even Jenna is being sweet about it."

"Good. I'm glad to hear it."

"Look, can you come to dinner with us tomorrow night?"

"Us?" Taylor lowered the volume on the television.

"Yes. All of us. Everyone wants to spend time with you."

"Okay."

"Seriously, Taylor, is it too weird?"

161

"Who cares?"

"I have no idea how I'll keep my paws off you during dinner."

"Sit next to me and sneak grabs." Taylor grinned excitedly.

"Also..."

"Yes?"

"They were cool with the idea of my living here."

"Why wouldn't they be? It's a perfect idea."

"Uh. How big is your house?"

"Why? You some kind of snob?" Taylor teased.

"Well?"

"Big. As big as yours, hot stuff."

"Oh, mine isn't nearly as big as yours, stud-man."

"We talkin' about my house?"

"Oh, sorry. Got sidetracked. Good. So, ah...I suppose I'll put my place up for sale, and set up a business here."

"Sounds good to me." Taylor finished the rest of beer then purred, "You up for phone sex?"

"I'll wait 'til everyone's asleep and call you back."

"Good." Taylor rubbed his crotch feeling how hard he'd already gotten just thinking about Owen.

"Okay. So, uh, I'll call you in a couple of hours, and tomorrow I'll pick you up."

"Okay."

"Were do you live?"

"You have a pen handy?" Taylor waited then gave Owen the address and directions.

"Right. Let me call you back later."

"I'll be here." Taylor hung up and then reclined on the chair, his hopes high for a happy ending.

Chapter Thirteen

Owen drove Jenna's Subaru to Taylor's place. It seemed strange since Owen had no idea what to expect, and having Jenna and Leah with him on his first visit to his intended place of abode was slightly scary. As he drew close, his fears were alleviated. The homes in the area were immense mansions with acres of land surrounding them. Pulling up into Taylor's drive, seeing him at his door waiting, Owen felt like a giddy schoolgirl. Realizing Taylor was waving them in, Owen shut the car and twisted to the back seat to the two women. "He wants us to come in."

"Cool!" Leah shouted, unbuckling her seatbelt.

As Jenna climbed out, she asked, "You said he was in construction? Christ, does he own the company?"

"No, his dad does." Owen led the way to a waiting Taylor, who had the door open for them.

"Come in. We have a minute." Taylor gestured for them to enter.

Owen pecked him on the cheek and then had a look around the living room. "Wow. Nice."

"Look, Daddy!" Leah raced to a wall of pictures. "It's Taylor on a horse!"

Under his breath Owen whispered to Taylor, "You are a cowboy. You devil."

Jenna stood behind Leah and admired the assortment of

photos with her.

"Now I'll never live it down," Taylor winked at him. "You guys want a tour before we go?"

Since they all did, Taylor waved his hand for them to follow, which they did eagerly.

Staying in the background as Taylor showed them each room and explained his personal touches in the design, Owen couldn't imagine loving Taylor any more than he did at that moment.

At one point, Leah asked, "When my Dad lives here, can I stay overnight sometimes?"

"If your mom says it's okay, it's my pleasure," Taylor responded.

"Mom?" Leah asked, as if she needed to sleep there that night.

"Your father hasn't even moved in yet, Leah." Jenna then added, "Of course you can."

After Leah's cheers of excitement, Taylor asked, "Everyone hungry?"

"Starved," Owen replied, giving Taylor a sly look, telling him he wasn't only hungry for food.

Jenna obviously noticed it for she admonished, "Behave you two."

"Moi?" Owen pushed his hand to his chest in denial.

"I'll get my coat." Taylor left them standing in the living room by the door.

When he had, Jenna whispered to Owen, "Damn. He's amazing."

"I know. Believe it? Me? With a guy like that?"

A strange look came into Jenna's eyes. "You know, Owen, you do have something to offer a partner. You're not the loser you think you are."

"Obviously I didn't have enough to offer you," Owen replied, checking to see where Leah was. She was back ogling the picture of Taylor on a horse.

"You were gay!" she hissed, looking back at her

daughter. "Do you really regret our divorce and being with Taylor?"

"No, but I do regret what our separating has done to Leah."

When Taylor returned they shut up. He paused, zipping his brown leather jacket and asked, "Am I interrupting something?"

"No, no…" both Owen and Jenna sang in a chorus.
The minute Leah noticed him, she grabbed Taylor's hand and begged, "Tell me about the horses."

Smiling sweetly at her, Taylor said, "Well, my daddy has a ranch in Texas…"

Owen and Jenna exchanged smiles as they headed out to the car and to dinner.

Chapter Fourteen

Taylor packed his bag for his Sunday night flight back to LA. When the phone rang he thought it must be Owen. Rushing to grab it before his answering machine picked up, Taylor said, "Hello?"

"Taylor, it's Landon. I'm sorry to call you so late on a Sunday, but you told me you were flying out to LA again."

"Hey, Landon. No, I'm glad you called. So? What about the job? Can you use me?"

"Are you sure you want to come work for us? I mean, your father has the biggest damn construction firm in the States. I can't pay you that amount of money."

Taylor sat down on his bed, checking his watch. "Look, Landon, I'm sick to death of traveling every month. And you know I get tired of my father's pressure. It's non-stop. Now I'm not saying I can't work under pressure—"

"I know what you're saying, Taylor. Believe me, we won't do what your dad does to you."

"Landon, I love your company. You guys are honest, hard-working, and local. Okay, the jobs are smaller, but they don't require me being gone so much."

"I can't believe Taylor Madison wants to settle down. You always came across as a free spirit. Did some woman finally rope you?"

"No, Landon, some man did." Taylor waited, wondering

if now the job offer would vanish.

"What? What did you say?"

"I said a man did. Look, Landon, I'm gay. You not offering me the position now?"

"Gay? You? Taylor I never met a more masculine man in my life."

"Forget it, Landon, I've a plane to catch." Taylor went to hang up.

"Wait! Wait a minute, Taylor. Stop being so impulsive. Just because you're gay doesn't mean I'm not interested in hiring you. Christ, they don't come better than you in the field. I'll snap you up. I don't care if you wear fucking dresses and undergo a sex change!"

Taylor started laughing. "Ah, no problem, I'm not doing either of those."

"It's the salary I'm worried about, Taylor. That's all."

"Okay, look, how about this? I'll call you when I'm back in LA. At the moment I've got to catch a flight. Let me go and when I have more time we'll discuss it in detail. But I've got a nice nest egg already, so I'm not too worried, you know. My house and car are paid for, what the hell do I need to earn so much for?"

"Am I hearing you straight?"

"Never mind, Landon. It's about priorities and money ain't always top on my list."

"Okay, Taylor. You call me. We'll negotiate. I want you on our team. That's not even a consideration."

"And no traveling, right?"

"No. All local work. Worst is overnight once in a while in Wyoming, but no longer than a day's drive."

"Okay. That's all I need to know." Taylor looked at his watch again. "I gotta run. Thanks for getting back to me, Landon. I'll call you once I'm in LA and have more time."

"Looking forward to it."

Taylor hung up, grabbed his bag and raced out of his house.

Owen checked the time. Standing at the doorway of Jenna's house, he wondered if he should call Taylor to make sure he was on his way.

"Daddy?"

Twisting over his shoulder, he found Leah standing behind him. "Yes?"

"Will you buy me a pony?"

Stifling a laugh, Owen crouched down to be eye to eye with her. "Ah...I can't right now. But we can go ride a pony this summer. Is that okay?"

"Leah," Jenna piped in, "we can't get you a pony."

Hearing a car horn, Owen stood up and found Taylor's truck parked out front. "Gotta go." He kissed Leah's cheek, waving to Jenna.

"Call when you get there," Jenna shouted.

"I will." Owen rushed outside as Taylor opened the back of the truck for him to put his suitcase in. "You're late."

"I know. Get in." Taylor hurried to the driver's door. Once they were on their way, Taylor explained, "I got a phone call right before I left the house."

"Oh?"

"Yeah. There's this local company that's been trying to get me on as their project manager for ages. Jordon Enterprises. You hear of it?"

"No, but go ahead." Owen held on as Taylor hit the gas when they met the highway ramp, trying to get them to the airport on time.

"Well, the owner, Landon Jordan offered me a job. No more traveling."

"Oh?" Owen felt his heart skip a beat. "And?"

"Well, I'm gonna take it. But I got to let dad know. Let him down easy."

"Okay. Well, that solves two problems."

"Two?" Taylor flipped on his radar detector and then flew over the speed limit.

"Yes. Our being apart all the time, and you not being under your father's thumb."

A low chuckle came out of Taylor as a reply.

~

Running with their bags, Taylor felt the sweat break out on his forehead from being overheated with his coat on in the terminal. They left their bags at check-in and raced to the security point.

"Shit. We won't have time for a drink. I'm sorry, Owen." Taylor took off his jacket and stuffed it into a tub on the conveyer belt. As Taylor emptied his pockets next, into another small plastic box, he said, "Bet they pat me down."

"Christ, if I were a security guard, I'd want to rub all over you."

"Here goes." Taylor walked through the metal detector, expecting to be stopped. When he wasn't Taylor spun around, rolling with laughing when Owen had his hands raised up in the air as the uniformed man gave him a good rubdown.

Meeting Owen's eyes, Taylor shook his head in hilarity. Once Owen had made his way through to where Taylor was collecting his belongings, Owen breathed, "Wow. That was unbelievable."

"Your next fantasy? Airport security guard and passenger?" Taylor shoved his wallet back into his pocket.

"No, but how about cop and criminal?" Owen's eyes lit up.

"What am I going to do with you?" Taylor kept laughing. "All right, let's get a move on."

Jogging to their gate, they finally caught their breath when they made it in time and joined the small lingering line that was left to board the flight to LA.

Once they were seated, Taylor exclaimed, "I'm roasting."

"Take off your shirt," Owen dared.

"Shut up. You just are the horniest mother-fucker on the planet."

"Duh." Owen shook his head as if he were stating the

obvious. "Oh, by the way. I got the lube." He took the tube out of his jacket pocket to show Taylor.

"Flying united again?" Taylor laughed.

Owen blinked his eyes, then replied, "Good one! Very good."

Once everyone had taken their seats and they were moving away from the terminal, Taylor began rehearsing the conversation in his head he needed to have with his dad when he got to LA. It wasn't going to be easy.

As if Owen noticed his pensive mood, he asked, "You okay?"

"Yeah, fine. So, another bout of sex in that tiny closet space?"

"Are you not up for it?"

"I'm always up for it."

Owen found the blue flannel blanket and ripped off the plastic cover.

"I've created a monster," Taylor laughed as Owen spread out the material over both their laps, quickly reaching over for a feel between Taylor's legs.

"Yes. You have. You've made me a sex fiend."

"Don't blame me for your deviant behavior." Taylor listened to the announcements about safety, which he could recite by heart.

"I do. You corrupted me. I was a mild-mannered accountant, and you turned me into a cowboy-craving sex maniac."

"I did all that. Then I must be amazing."

"Oh, you are…believe me."

Taylor closed his eyes as Owen massaged between his legs more aggressively.

As the nose of the plane pointed up once more, Taylor's cock tried to do the same thing in the confines of his tight blue jeans. Under the blanket, Owen boldly opened Taylor's zipper and reached inside. When Owen's hand touched his skin, Taylor bit back a groan that would undoubtedly alert someone nearby that they were doing naughty things.

Straddling his legs, Taylor's head felt light as both he and the jet floated above the clouds. Knowing his entire cock was now protruding from his pants, Taylor peeked down. Seeing the blanket appearing like a pup-tent and movement from Owen's hand which was jerking him off at the moment, Taylor begged the seatbelt light to flick off so he could cover up the action with the tray. When that didn't happen soon enough, he grabbed the in-flight magazine from the seat pocket and opened it up to shield the sex act from prying eyes.

"If you keep that up, you'll make me come, Owen," Taylor whispered.

"It just feels so good," Owen whispered back.

"I'll get sperm on my clothing."

"Use this." Owen handed him the plastic cover from the blanket with his free hand.

"Are you outta your mind?" Taylor felt his body shiver as Owen was intent on making him come where he sat. "Owen! I can't hold on." Feeling it rush up on him before he could prevent it, Taylor snatched the plastic and whipped it under the blanket quickly, trying his best to catch what was destined to come out.

Never in his wildest dreams did Taylor imagine he would be ejaculating in his seat, with a plane full of passengers all completely oblivious to the deed. And it washed over him like a tsunami. It was so daring, so naughty, Taylor thought he would combust with the inferno coming from his loins. His body tensing up, his teeth clenching, Taylor came.

~

Owen was literally on fire watching Taylor. The expression on Taylor's face, the fact that this fantastic hunk was coming right there, in public... It was so taboo and stimulating, Owen almost did the same thing. And if he could he would.

As Taylor held back his grunting from the intensity,

Owen stopped moving his hand and waited. No one had a clue. They were still climbing in altitude, so there wasn't anyone walking the aisles or looking around. Most passengers were reading, listening to music from the headphones, or sleeping.

Taylor dared to look down at his lap to see what actually was going on under the blanket. Owen watched curiously, noticing Taylor had done well catching the sperm in the plastic bag. "Wow. Good job."

Wrapping it up, Taylor handed it to Owen, saying, "It's yours to deal with, dear. You made it. You take it."

Stifling a laugh, Owen took the milky parcel and stared at it in awe as Taylor adjusted himself under the blanket, getting decent again.

"What the hell should I do with it?" Owen asked, still restraining the urge to burst out laughing.

"Use it on your damn ravioli, I don't know." After Taylor put the magazine back into the pocket, he raised the blanket up as if checking his pants to see if everything was kosher underneath.

"Well? Are you covered with it?" Owen held up the package.

Taylor nudged him to put it down lower. "Yes, I'm fine. Now do something with that."

"What?" Owen laughed out loud finally. "The seatbelt sign is lit."

"Put it in the barf bag."

"Oh, good idea." Owen dug around his seat pocket, pulling out a paper bag. After he stuffed the gooey contents in it, then wrapped it up tightly, Owen asked, "You think they'll see it's used and toss it?"

"Yeah. Don't worry."

Once Owen had tucked it into the pocket of the seat, he leaned on Taylor and hissed, "You came on the plane in the seat. What club does that qualify you for?"

"The 'Insane Peoples' Club. You nut!"

"Oh, come on, you didn't even stop me."

"I couldn't. You had me too far gone."

"You're the one who said you'd suck me with your head under the damn blanket, remember? So? Do I still get mine?" Owen grinned wickedly. When he felt Taylor reaching under the blanket for him, Owen panicked. "No! Not here. In the head."

"Oh? Is that right? Coming in the airplane seat is good for some, but not for you?" Taylor managed to get his hand into Owen's pants.

"Holy crap. I can't do this. I swear, I won't be able to do it here."

"Shut up and close your damn eyes."

"But the stewardess will come around with the cart."

"Not while we're so damn turbulent. No one's going nowhere."

"Oh, my god..." Owen freaked out when Taylor lowered his zipper. Looking down, seeing the blanket wasn't concealing them completely, Owen ripped a magazine from the pocket, opening it, and covered his lap. The minute Taylor had his cock out of his jeans and was stroking it, Owen forgot the fear and panic and melted into the sensation of, well, his cock being stroked by a master.

Blinking his eyes open, Owen asked, "What can I use? We already used the plastic thing."

"Tear a piece of that magazine."

"What? Deface the magazine?"

"Owen, for cryin' out loud."

As slowly as he could, Owen ripped a page out, trying not to make any noise. Stuffing it under the blanket, he placed it where he thought he would shoot come. "This is so insane."

"Oh? More insane than when you did it to me?" Taylor increased the speed of his jerking.

In reflex, Owen stretched out his legs, spreading them wide as they burrowed under the seat in front of him in the tight space. Closing his eyes, trying to find the daring humor in this insanity, Owen couldn't believe when he felt like he could actually come under these conditions. Taylor had turned in his seat, literally blocking any view with his broad back of what was going on. As Taylor's hand squeezed and yanked on Owen's cock, Owen gave in, coming, in the damn seat of the plane.

Feeling Taylor's hand slow, and then stop, Owen dreaded looking under the blanket. "Here we go. Fingers crossed."

As Owen removed the magazine page, Taylor retrieved the old barf bag from the seat to add the new contents.

There, covering a lipstick model's painted face, was Owen's sperm. "Think she liked it?"

"She's the type that would throw it up after eating it. Here, put it into the damn bag."

Owen folded it into fours, sliding it into the paper sack. As Taylor wrapped up the vomit bag once more, Owen tucked himself in and zipped up. Once they felt as if they had completed that obscene act, they looked at each other in amazement. "I can't believe we did that." Owen shook his head.

"Me, neither. I swear we'll get caught one of these days and fined or something."

"Well, soon we won't be on a plane every week. We'll have the luxury of your bed."

"True. Our airplane screwing days are numbered."

"Will you miss it?" Owen smiled sadly.

"Yes and no."

The seatbelt sign finally shut off and the drink cart began its slow move down the aisle as several people stood to stretch their legs or use the toilet. Right after they ordered their drinks, a very slender, effeminate male sauntered close to their aisle.

As Owen watched him curiously, it seemed the man was lingering there for a reason. The moment the attendant moved on, he leaned down to whisper to them, "I'm insanely jealous of you boys." The lisp was very pronounced, and Owen could tell he was gay and proud, in many ways. "You two should be ashamed of yourselves." But he batted his lashes and smiled as he said it.

Leaning over Taylor's lap so he could whisper, Owen asked, "Does everyone know?"

"Oh, I doubt it, honey. Just me. But I couldn't keep my eyes off either one of you. Ah, interested in a little ménage in the bathroom?"

After a deep low chuckle, Taylor replied, "No, darlin', I'm afraid we're exclusive."

"Oh, too bad for me. It was fun watching you boys anyhow. Bye!"

As he wiggled off, Owen gasped at Taylor and exclaimed, "Shit. I can't believe he knew."

"He's gay, Owen. No one else would know."

Gulping his wine, Owen said, "Man, I am glad we'll soon be done flying. The novelty has left. It's really draining."

"It is, babe. And soon it'll be history."

Owen tapped Taylor's beer bottle with his wine glass, saying, "Amen to that."

~

The long flight and drive was finally behind them. Once inside Owen's home, they unpacked their bags and managed to eat a light snack.

Taylor sat with the phone and made that dreaded call to his father. Without Taylor asking him, Owen had given him privacy and left to watch television in the den while Taylor sat on Owen's bed and used the phone on the nightstand.

"Taylor?"

"Yes, it's me, Pop."

"Good. I wanted to talk to you."

"Yeah, I wanted to talk to you, too." Taylor knew it would be a confrontation, dreading it.

"I've sent Noah out. He'll be on the site in the morning. You show him where you left off. You got that?"

"I do. Now, I got something to tell you. I'm going to

work for Jordon Construction in Denver."

"You what? You out of your mind?"

"No. Pop, I'm sick of traveling. I don't want to do it anymore. Landon said I can do all his local work in Colorado. So, after I get Noah sorted on this project, I'm done." Silence followed. It was long, strained, and annoying. "Are you there, or did you go take a damn shit?" Taylor shouted in anger.

"I'm here. Taylor, you know you're gonna take a huge cut in pay."

"I do know."

"And you're going to do that for some homo-lover you found? You sure you know what you're doing?"

"I do. I swear, Pop, he's the best thing that's ever happened to me."

"You've never settled, Taylor. You flit from one sex-partner to the next."

"Bullshit! That's complete crap, Pop, and you know it. I haven't even seen anyone since Will. And that was ages ago. Where on earth do you get your gossip from?"

"Caleb. He says you flirt with all the boys on the site. He told me you're promiscuous and I should give you a lecture about AIDS."

Taylor counted to ten in his head because he was about to combust. "Pop, you sure you can believe Caleb? Talk about a string of bad relationships? Caleb screws more bimbo prostitutes that line the streets of hooker-town, than there are grains of sand on Redondo Beach. Pop, don't listen to him. He's the equivalent of a male whore. The boy's not stable."

"All right, stop bad-mouthin' your brother."

"Stop—" Taylor bit his lip and then calmed down. "You tell me to stop bad-mouthing Caleb, but you listen to his crap about me."

"Forget about that. Now, about this job over at Jordon's...what's he paying you?"

"None of your damn business. I'm givin' you my notice."

"Now, wait. Don't be hasty. You're too hasty."

"Pop, you need me to travel. Ya got no business for me to do in Colorado."

"Now, that's where you're wrong. I can do business there. Do you want to set us up a nice office to conduct local work for our company?"

Taylor choked in surprise. "You mean…"

"Compete with fucking Jordon. Don't give him our best boy."

Taylor couldn't believe what he was hearing. "You talkin' about me?"

"Yeah, who do you think I'm talking about? Caleb? You! I'm talking about you."

"How the hell do I set up an office in Denver?"

"I'll send some boys over to help you. You just go out and pick out a nice place. We'll buy the building and do it up right."

"You sure? There may not be as much local work as you think."

"Whatever it is, you do it."

"No more traveling? Promise?" Taylor knew there had to be a catch.

"Promise. You won't go anyway, if I ask you."

"No, I won't."

"So, I won't ask you."

"Okay. Let me wrap this LA job up this week, and get Noah up to scratch."

"When ya get back in Denver, call me. I'll send out some people there to help you."

"I can't believe you're doing this, Pop."

"Well, you were right, Taylor. You're the one I can count on. Your brothers are useless."

"Thanks. I mean it."

"No problem."

"Oh, before you go…" Taylor could hear Owen in the next room but knew he was busy.

"What?"

"Look, this man, my partner, he's got a ten-year-old daughter from a previous marriage who's nuts about horses."

"Bring her by."

"Yeah?" Taylor was shocked.

"Yeah, bring her by, and we'll show her a good time."

"Thanks, Pop. You really are okay when ya wanna be."

"I suppose from you that's high praise. You just keep me in the loop. Tell me what you're doing."

"I will. See ya, Pop." Taylor hung up and tried to believe everything he'd just heard.

~

Owen was sitting in the den with his old high school yearbook on his lap, reminiscing about the bad old days just to kill time until Taylor finished his phone call. Owen looked up as Taylor came into the room, sitting next to him on the couch.

"Is that yours?" Taylor asked.

"Yes. Look at me back then." Owen handed Taylor the book with his photo.

"You're not ugly, Owen. I can see the potential in you a mile away."

"You're sweet. Thanks. So, how did the call go?"

"Real good. Pop wants me to open an office in Denver and get into the local construction scene there."

"Are you serious?"

"I am. So, no more traveling, and no cut in pay."

Owen dove down on him, shoving the book to the floor, lying on top of him. "I am so happy for you."

"So, it's just a matter of time for you to sell and move."

"Yes. Exactly."

"Meanwhile, Noah is coming out this week and taking over for me. So, this is my last week here."

"It's okay. I'll make sure the house is priced to sell." Owen stared down into Taylor's bright blue eyes. "Can this really work?"

"Yes. It can." Taylor wrapped his arms around Owen's

waist. "My father invited you and your daughter down to the ranch. I told him how much she loved horses."

Owen almost choked with emotion. "Leah will die. Oh, you will make her day."

"She have a fantasy about cowboys as well?" Taylor wriggled under him.

"Who doesn't?" Owen wriggled back, then connected to Taylor's mouth. After a long passionate kiss, Owen sat up and said, "Looks like our Mile High days have reached an end."

"Yeah, but what a nice story to tell the grandkids."

Seeing that mischievous twinkle in Taylor's eyes, Owen began laughing. "I adore you, you know that?"

"And I love you, Owen Braydon."

Owen kissed him again, then said, "Happily ever after? Did we do it?"

"We sure did, partner! Yee haw!"

Cracking up with laughter, Owen rolled with Taylor on the couch, shouting, "Ride em', cowboy!"

The End

About the Author

Award-winning author G.A. Hauser was born in Fair Lawn, New Jersey, USA and attended university in New York City. She moved to Seattle, Washington where she worked as a patrol officer with the Seattle Police Department. In early 2000 G.A. moved to Hertfordshire, England where she began her writing in earnest and published her first book, In the Shadow of Alexander. Now a full-time writer, G.A. has written over fifty novels, including several best-sellers of gay fiction and is an Honorary Board Member of Gay American Heroes for her support of the foundation. For more information on other books by G.A., visit the author at her official website. www.authorgahauser.com

G.A. has won awards from All Romance eBooks for Best Author 2009, Best Novel 2008, *Mile High*, and Best Author 2008, Best Novel 2007, *Secrets and Misdemeanors*, Best Author 2007.

Other works by G.A. Hauser:

Capital Games

Let the games begin...

Former Los Angeles Police officer Steve Miller has gone from walking a beat in the City of Angels to joining the rat race as an advertising executive. He knows how cut-throat the industry can be, so when his boss tells him that he's in direct competition with a newcomer from across the pond for a coveted account he's not surprised...then he meets Mark Richfield.

Born with a silver spoon in his mouth and fashion-model good looks, Mark is used to getting what he wants. About to be married, Mark has just nailed the job of his dreams. If the determined Brit could just steal the firm's biggest account right out from under Steve Miller, his life would be perfect.

When their boss sends them together to the Arizona desert for a team-building retreat the tension between the two dynamic men escalates until in the heat of the moment their uncontrollable passion leads them to a sexual experience that neither can forget.

Will Mark deny his feelings and follow through with marriage to a women he no longer wants, or will he realize in time that in the game of love, sometimes you have to let go and lose yourself in order to *really* win.

Secrets and Misdemeanors

When having to hide your love is a crime...

After losing his wife to his best friend and former law partner, David Thornton couldn't imagine finding love again. With his divorce behind him, he wanted only to focus on his job and two children. But then something happened, making David realize that despite believing he had everything he needed, there was someone he desperately wanted—Lyle Wilson.

Young and determined, Lyle arrived in Los Angeles without a penny in his pocket. Before long, however, the sexy construction worker nailed a job remodeling the old office building that held the prestigious Thornton Law Firm. Little did Lyle realize when he gazed upon the handsome and successful David Thornton for the first time that a door would be opened that neither man could close.

Will the two men succumb to the tangled web of societal pressures placed before them, hiding who they are and whom they love? Or will they reveal the truth and set themselves free?

Naked Dragon

Police Officer Dave Harris has just been assigned to one of the worst serial murder cases in Seattle history: The Dragon is hunting young Asian men. In order to solve the crime it's going to take a bit more than good old-fashioned police work. It's going to take handsome FBI Agent Robbie Taylor.

Robbie is an experienced Federal Agent with psychic abilities that allow him to enter the minds of others. You can't hide your secrets and desires from someone that knows your every thought. Some think what Robbie has is a gift, others a skill, but when the mind you have to enter is that of a madman it can also be a curse.

As the corpses pile up and the tension mounts, so does the sexual attraction between the two men. Then a moment of passion leads to a secret affair. Will their love be the distraction that costs them the case and possibly even their lives? Or will the bond forged between them be the key to their survival?

The Kiss

Twenty-five year old actor Scott Epstein is no stranger to the modeling industry. He's done it himself between acting jobs. So when his sister, Claire, casts him in a chewing-gum commercial with the famous British model, Ian Sullivan, he doesn't ask any questions. He's a professional. He'll show up, hit his mark, say his lines, and collect his paycheck. Right?

Ian Sullivan is used to making heads turn. Stunningly handsome, he's accustomed to provocative photo shoots where sex sells everything from perfume to laundry soap. Ian was thrilled when Claire Epstein cast him in the new Minty gum commercial. He has to kiss his co-star on screen? No problem. Until he finds out Scott is the one he has to kiss!

Never before has a commercial featured two men, kissing on screen. Claire knows that the advertisement will be ground-breaking, and Scott knows that his sister needs his performance to be perfect. As the filming progresses and the media circus begins around the controversial advertisement, the chemistry between Ian and Scott heats up and the two men quite simply burn up the screen. Is it all an act? Or, have Ian and Scott entered into a clandestine affair that will lead them to love?

For Love and Money

Handsome Dr. Jason Philips, the heir to a vast fortune, had followed his heart and pursued his dream of becoming a physician. Ewan P. Gallagher had a different dream. Acting in local theater, the talented twenty-year-old was determined to be a famous success.

As fate would have it, Jason happened to be working in casualty one night when Ewan was admitted as a patient. Jason was more than flattered and surprisingly aroused by the younger man's obvious attraction to him. The two men entered into a steamy affair finding love, until their ambitions pulled them apart.

Now, one year later and stuck in a sham of a marriage that he entered into only to preserve his inheritance, Jason is filled with regret. Caught between obligation and freedom, duty and desire, Jason finds that he can no longer deny his passion. He plans to win Ewan, Hollywood's newest rising star, back!

The G.A. Hauser Collection
Single Titles

Unnecessary Roughness
Hot Rod
The Diamond Stud
Games Men Play
Born to Please
Got Men?
Heart of Steele
All Man
Julian
Black Leather Phoenix
London, Bloody, London
In The Dark and What Should Never Be, Erotic Short Stories
Mark and Sharon (formally titled A Question of Sex)
A Man's Best Friend
It Takes a Man
The Physician and the Actor
For Love and Money
The Kiss
Naked Dragon
Secrets and Misdemeanors
Capital Games
Giving Up the Ghost
To Have and To Hostage
Love you, Loveday
The Boy Next Door
When Adam Met Jack
Exposure
The Vampire and the Man-eater
Murphy's Hero
Mark Antonious deMontford
Prince of Servitude
Calling Dr Love
The Rape of St. Peter
The Wedding Planner
Going Deep

Made in the USA
Lexington, KY
22 September 2011